ALSO BY I

CW01498079

Alexander King

THE SECRET WEAPON

COLD WAR

MOST WANTED

POWER MOVE

ENEMY LINES

SMOKE SCREEN

SPY RING

WAR MACHINE

Alexander King Prequels

WHISKEY & ROSES

VANQUISH

KING'S RANSOM

KING'S REIGN

SCOURGE

Tom Walker

Killer Instinct

Holy Water

Blind Pass

Deliverance

The Wrong Man

Black Market

Lawson Raines

WHEN THE MAN COMES AROUND

SHOOTING STAR

Saint Nick

SAINT NICK

SAINT NICK 2

WAR
MACHINE

WAR
MACHINE

For my readers. Thank you for always showing up.

The world is full of monsters with friendly faces and angels with scars.

— HEATHER BREWER

WAR
MACHINE

PROLOGUE

———

"Mijo, I told you, you can't be in here," Lucia told her son Santiago.

Santiago knew his mother was going to say it. She'd said it a thousand times over the last couple of years that she had been cleaning the Ford House office building in the capital of the United States. She was worried to death that she would lose her job. Overly worried if you asked Santiago, but his mother worried about everything. She had the entire thirteen years he'd been alive.

"Relax, Mom. Nobody actually cares that I am here."

"You know that's not true. Several workers here have complained about you being here. This is a federal building, mijo. Lots of important things go on here. I've told you this. Things that no one in the world is supposed to know about.

1

You sneaking around the halls and in and out of the break rooms to get snacks makes people nervous."

"Everyone knows me here, Mom. They don't care."

"You don't have to deal with the complaints. There are hundreds of staff members and workers here. Not even a fraction of them know who you are. What do you want, anyway? There is a lot going on in the city today with the inauguration. You should be home."

Santiago gave his mother his patented grin that he knew she couldn't resist. "I just wanted to see my momma. Is that so bad?"

Lucia leaned into his hug. "Just go now, okay?" she said with a smile. "I have to work. And I don't need to be worrying about you, worrying all the people here."

"All right. I'll be at Shane's house."

"Okay. Straight there, then straight home. You understand? I don't want you out and about today. Too many people and too much going on."

"Okay, Mom," he said with a laugh. "Why the extra men here today? That because of the inauguration too?"

"Extra men?"

"Yeah, I tried to go out to get my iPad, but I just went back up when I stepped into the lobby. At least seven or eight more dudes here now than there were earlier when I got here."

"I don't know, Santi. Nothing here has anything to do with the inauguration. Maybe someone important is meeting with one of the Senators. Either way, you shouldn't be here. Okay? Promise me you'll stay away."

Santi walked over and gave his mother a hug. He was already taller than she was, but at less than five-feet, that wasn't saying much.

"I love you. Now get. Text me when you get to your friend's house."

"Okay. Talk soon."

Santiago let go of his mother, grabbed a pack of peanuts from the counter, and walked out of the break room. He headed down the hallway and pressed the button for the elevator. The break room was in the basement, so he needed to go up a floor to make his way out of the building. One floor was about all he could take of the elevator music. He was not a fan of smooth jazz, or whatever they called it. Wasn't sure how any human could be. It didn't have a beat. Not like rap music. He supposed maybe it was a generational thing.

The elevator dinged and the door separated. He took one step out and froze. There were three men in tactical gear, guns on their hips, staring right at him, about fifty feet away in front of the entrance. When they saw him, they squared up. He didn't like their posture. All he could hear in his head was his mother telling him how his presence in the building made people nervous. Were these guys here for him? He'd dodged them earlier. Had they been waiting for him to come back down the entire time?

Whatever the case with the men actually was, every fiber of his being was telling him he could not walk toward them. So, he picked up his foot, put it in reverse, and backed into the elevator.

"Hey, come on out here. We need to talk to you," a man's voice boomed from the lobby.

Santiago tapped the button for the top floor, then started spamming the "close door" button below. He didn't stop tapping it as fast as he could while the door began closing.

"Hey, wait a minute," the man from the hallway shouted again.

Santiago pecked harder on the button. Just as one of the men became visible, the slit in the door closed and kept them away from him. He shuffled and put his back against the wall behind him. The elevator shook and began rising. He wasn't sure what he was going to do from the top floor, but it was the only move he had to get away from the men.

"What the hell did I do?" he asked the empty elevator. "Why do they want me?"

Santiago obviously had no idea if they wanted him or not, but he made the rash decision that it wasn't worth sticking around to find out. Now, he would just have to hide. He would wait all day if he had to. Eventually, they would leave if they couldn't find him, right?

It was all he had.

The elevator reached the top floor. He hadn't been to this level in a long time. The only thing he knew about it was that some of the more *important* people in the building had offices up there. According to his mother, anyway. The door opened and he walked out into the hall. It was still pretty early, so there wasn't much going on. He stepped out and heard some movement on his left, so he immediately turned and walked right.

All along the hallway were closed doors. He heard someone talking behind him. He picked up the pace. His head was twisting left and right, hoping to find someplace to hide. He glanced back over his shoulder and saw a man in a suit step out into the hallway. His back was to Santiago so he hadn't seen him. Yet. All the office doors were closed around him. He looked back again and the man started to turn. Santiago was about to freak out, when he finally noticed that the door at the end of the hall was ajar.

Santiago planted his back foot and sprang forward into a sprint. He got to the door, made himself skinny, and jumped sideways through it, making sure the door didn't move. Once inside he saw a grand office. The wall at the other end of the room was all windows. He could see the sun rising over Washington, D.C. His pause inside the door allowed him to hear that the man, and whoever he was speaking to, were definitely moving toward him out in the hallway.

Santiago looked past the fancy coffee maker on the table to search for a place to hide in case his bad luck was that this was the man in the suit's office. Beyond the table there was a large cabinet displaying artifacts of all sorts. Beneath the display were cabinets. Santiago was skinny. He knew if nothing was in there, he would fit. He crossed his fingers and said a quick prayer as he ran over to it.

Out in the hallway, the voices grew closer. The cracked door to that office must have been open because it was the office of the man in the suit. Santiago bent down and pulled the handle on the door of the cabinet. When it popped open, he was relieved to find nothing inside. He made himself small and slithered inside like a snake. The cabinet was long, so there was actually plenty of room for his skinny frame. He curled back up to shut the door behind him, just as he heard the man enter the office.

Santiago laid flat on his back, began to try and steady his breathing, and went as still as he could as his heart raced. As the footsteps grew closer, his mind searched for a reason those men might be after him. His mom did say that he was making people nervous. But to respond with that many armed men was a bit of an overreaction. He thought for a minute that maybe he had just let his mother make him paranoid. Maybe no one cared about him at all.

Just when Santiago had all but talked himself into exiting the cabinet and apologizing to the man in the suit, he heard the door shut, and the man began talking to someone.

"Are you sure we have everything in place?"

The man paused. Santiago realized he was on the phone.

"And countermeasures for local military, you're sure they won't be able to make it into the city?"

Local military?

"This is it. Twenty years of exhaustive planning and maneuvering. All for this day. As soon as we've crippled the defenses, we have to seize control. We only get one shot at this."

Santiago had no idea what the man was talking about, but it didn't sound good. Hopefully the man was talking about some other country and he just missed the first part of the man's conversation.

"People are going to remember this as a before and after this day kind of date. The United States of America will never be the same."

Santiago might not be old and wise, but it was clear that whatever this man was talking about wasn't good. In fact, Santiago, all of a sudden, felt terrified. What in the world could this man be talking about? What could ever change America forever?

Santiago swallowed hard and did his best to keep his fear under control. If something big was going on, and this man found him in his cabinet, listening, the men downstairs would certainly be after him then. He knew he was going to have to stay quiet, and stay hidden for as long as this man was in his office. Even if it took all day. Or longer.

CHAPTER ONE

A BONE-CHILLING COLD FRONT HAD MOVED IN ACROSS MOST of the northeastern portion of the United States over the last week. Lots of snow had fallen. Even more ice. Most of the Washington, D.C. area had been in a sort of paralysis. So much so that in a rare move, government officials had decided to move the presidential inauguration indoors. It was taking place at the Capitol Rotunda to be exact. The first to be indoors since Reagan's in 1985.

Alexander King didn't care much about any of it, except he was there. He didn't know the incoming president, but his old Navy SEAL buddy, Jonathan Vickers, was just about to become the vice president. Xander thought that was pretty cool. His date—his fiancée— the lovely Ms. Natalie Rockwell, was far more excited. She was actually a history buff. He'd known her for years, but that was a new fact to him. She, of course, gave him the speech about getting to know her better when he was dumbfounded by her love for the past. He supposed she had a point.

Despite the arctic temperatures, the sun was shining and it was a beautiful day. Xander wasn't fond of all the pageantry

7

that came along with the day. Humans had so many silly rituals. It seemed as though they were important to society, so they carried on and on. He just had to bite his tongue every time Natalie would gasp at a woman's beautiful dress, or hat. Men are from Mars, women are from Venus, and all that jazz.

Xander and Natalie had a unique perspective on the day. There weren't any more invitations to hand out, so the next VP, Jon, created a position for Xander. Xander being who he is lent the role credibility, so it was an easy sell. He was deemed part of security, but the secret, hidden in plain sight kind.

There were all kinds of well-to-do people lingering around the rotunda. Big tech, big automobile, big blah, blah, blah. But no one was more recognizable than the movie star on Xander's arm. Natalie's publicist begged her not to go. She was worried about the political backlash of attending such a polarizing event. Natalie didn't give a single shit. Xander admired that.

A perk of being "secret" security was that Xander was one of the only people in the building carrying a gun. He had a knife too, but Secret Service didn't seem as concerned about it. There were a lot of people in some of the media outlets who were worried something bad might happen at the inauguration. Natalie gave Xander a full rundown of all the events that had happened over the last couple of months that made some people nervous. Xander had heard some of it, some of it he hadn't. Security was so thick that Xander felt his gun was safe tucked down in its shoulder harness holster.

Xander and Natalie were seated in the rows beside and behind where the president was to be sworn in. This was rare ground, Natalie told him. As Xander looked around at the people sitting near him, he supposed she was right. There were at least three former presidents. A few big business men and women. Other people Xander didn't recognize, but was sure that they had contributed heavily to the president-elect's campaign fund.

Natalie leaned over and put her lips close to his ear. "This is *so* cool," she whispered. Barely containing herself. "This is history!"

Xander smiled. "And we know you love history."

She gave him a sour look. "Just because you don't care about any of this stuff doesn't mean you can ruin my fun."

Xander winked. "I wouldn't dare."

He watched his beautiful fiancée as her wide eyes took in all the sights. There were massive paintings all around the walls. Some people painted to be at war, some of men standing around a table, pilgrims and Indians, and even the dome over a hundred feet up was made into a mural. Everyone from George Washington to Poseidon had made it into that one. What a strange combination.

Xander's buddy, Jon, had just walked in a couple of minutes ago. The man at the podium was now introducing the next president of the United States. Music played as he and his family came walking down the hall. Xander zoned out, daydreaming of pizza or wings. It was noon after all. He doubted there would be anything good like pizza at the after-party though. Probably just some crummy finger foods. He'd beg Natalie to leave, but she would just shush him away. There were all kinds of music stars and so on set to play the big party at the Capital One Arena in town. She was excited for it. Xander's saving grace might be that Kyle and Sam were in town to join them at the party. The two of them, and Lawson Raines. Xander hadn't seen Lawson since their fast couple of days in Mexico City a few years ago. They'd stayed in close contact since. Lawson was a friend of some people in the incoming president's Secret Service team and they'd asked him to join the party. He was having lunch with Sam and Kyle at that very moment. Xander was looking forward to having a bourbon or six with him.

Before Xander and Natalie had been able to join the big shindig, Xander had to meet with Secret Service. That part, he didn't take lightly. If he was going to be there, he wanted to know the protocol if something bad did actually happen. They went over several key points about the Capitol Building, where the president would go if there was danger, and details of evacuation of all the important people. Xander thought they had a good plan. He also knew how chaos worked. He'd been there and done that many times. It was the improv after the protocols fail where heroes are forged. That all came back to their training. After an assassination attempt was too close for comfort a couple of months ago, a lot of people had questions there as well.

Xander obviously didn't know any of the individuals he was in the room with during this orientation, but they had all taken it very seriously. He also knew that if there were ever shenanigans involved with departments like the Secret Service or the CIA, that it was never the agents on the ground that caused them. It was the people in charge. Most of whom never had any business being in charge of anything. Much less, national security.

Natalie squeezed his arm as the president approached the podium and raised his right hand. It was go time. Natalie was geeking out. Xander did his best to see this inauguration from his favorite person's perspective, and zoned in on what the priest was saying before the swearing in was official.

That's when the lights went out.

CHAPTER TWO

THERE WAS A HUSH THAT FELL OVER THE CROWD WHEN THE lights went out. It was dead silent. The only light keeping the large room lit was from the windows. A massive sound bellowed from somewhere in the building and the generator whirred to life. The lights flickered at first, then became steady.

The crowd cheered.

"As I was saying," the priest said with a laugh.

The crowd joined him in the laugh. Natalie looked over at Xander nervously. He squeezed her hand and gave her a smile, but he hid the concern he was feeling. He didn't like the timing of the power outage. Even though it probably was just a coincidence, it made him uneasy.

The priest went on with his speech. It seemed as though it was winding down. It was time for the president-elect to repeat the words that would forever lock him into the history books. Just before he began repeating the priest's first sentence, the room once again went dark.

This time, the crowd gasped.

The hair on the back of Xander's neck stood on end.

"Swear him in!" Xander shouted. "Hurry up and swear him in!"

Murmuring began moving through the crowd.

Xander recognized the next voice he heard. It was Jon Vickers. "Yes, swear him in, now! He's not officially president. Security! Surround him!"

Xander began to move for the aisle but Natalie caught his arm. "You can't go!"

The last thing he wanted to do was leave her. He was her protector, then, and always. He was about to swear that oath to her in just a few short months when they were to be married. But he already swore an oath to protect his country. The president of the United States was his duty.

"I'll be right back. Just get down in your seat. This is probably nothing, but I have to help protect the president."

She understood history. She would understand what he had to do.

Natalie nodded and let go of his hand. "Be careful."

"Stay down."

By the time Xander made it down to the priest, the president was saying the last sentence of his oath. He was now officially the president of the United States.

Gunfire erupted outside the Capitol Building. It wasn't a single pistol. It wasn't even multiple pistols. It was a full-on orchestrated, military-style attack. Xander could hear it in the multitude of semi, and fully automatic gunfire. The power outage wasn't an act of Mother Nature.

It was an act of war.

That's when the now vice president of the United States, Jon Vickers caught Xander's eye. He knew what Xander knew. They were about to be in for the fight for their lives.

At first, the crowd, who hadn't been to war, didn't fully grasp what was happening. Even to Xander, who had been there and done that, it all seemed so surreal. With the moment they were all caught up in there in the Capitol rotunda, how could it not? How could this be happening?

Those questions would have to wait. Now, it was time to survive. Alexander King's survival instincts kicked in.

"Get the president to the safe room!" Xander shouted. "Ten of you! All of you surround him and stay together! Go now! The rest of security stay here with me!"

The room full of people then began to panic.

Jon looked over. "Listen to the man!" he shouted. Then spoke to Xander. "How many men do we have total?"

"Eighteen inside. Twenty more in the halls and at the entrances. We need to get everyone to the House Chamber. The briefing earlier said they installed bulletproof doors. Get someone who knows how to lead them there and can do it fast."

"My chief of staff," Jon said as he turned away.

"Everyone please try to calm down!" the president shouted as he was being escorted to safety. "Please! Listen to the gentlemen! They can help you get out of here safely!"

That helped quiet people for a moment. However, the quieter they became, the louder the gunfire outside. And it was getting closer. Then an explosion boomed in the distance. That was when the fear finally set in for the crowd. Another explosion farther away sounded, then another. Xander's stomach dropped.

Jon stood on one of the chairs. He pointed to the small, dark-haired woman down beside him. Then he just lifted her up with him. "Listen to me! Please! This is Sasha! She is going to lead you out of here, and over to the House Chamber. The doors are bulletproof there! You will be safe! Follow her!"

Xander knew that didn't mean they would be safe. But it was better than nothing.

Jon pointed to the door on the left side of the rotunda.

"Follow her to that door! We have plenty of security! You will be okay!"

Sasha jumped down and jogged for the door. The crowd moved quickly behind her. Xander stepped up on the chair beside him and searched a few rows back for Natalie. When he found her, the look on her face terrified him. The first thing that popped into his mind was, *what if this is the last time I ever see her alive?* His stomach rolled, but he put on a brave face.

"I'm staying with you!" she shouted.

Xander only half heard her over the crowd, but he could make out what she was saying by reading her lips. Xander shook his head. Then he mouthed the words, "It's not safe here."

Before she could protest, the door at the far end of the rotunda burst inward. Gunfire instantly erupted.

"Go!" Xander shouted to Natalie as he pulled his Glock from the holster beneath his suit jacket. "I'll find you!"

Xander didn't wait for a response, he whipped his head around until he saw the men who were escorting the president. He knew that from the gunmen's perspective when they entered the rotunda, that it would be obvious to see that was the president who was being escorted by the men. That's why they were instantly firing in that direction.

Xander jumped off the chair and grabbed Jon by the collar. Jon had been carrying as well, and already had his pistol in his hand. The chaos that erupted seemed like a movie. The unarmed patrons were in a frenzy. There was screaming, crying, gunfire, and people running around like mad trying to save themselves.

Xander pulled one security guard by the sleeve, toward the row of attending former presidents. "Protect the presidents!"

The man continued in their direction, pulling another

guard along with him. Xander and Jon stayed low. He was leading Jon away from the chaos that was moving toward where the president was being escorted. His goal was to make it around the other side of the crowd and ambush the gunmen who'd made their way into the rotunda. Xander didn't have time to give what was happening any thought. If he survived, he could worry about that later. And though every ounce of his soul wanted to be beside Natalie, he had to do whatever he could to save the president.

Xander's biggest concern was that it was already too late for that.

CHAPTER THREE

As Xander and Jon moved around the panicking crowd, Xander watched as more and more gunmen poured into the room. They must have moved through the twenty-some guards outside the rotunda with ease. No matter how focused Xander was on the moment, he couldn't help his brain when it leapt to conclusions such as just how big and coordinated was this attack? Big, and hyper-coordinated was the only answer that came back.

As he rounded a wave of people, he raised his Glock. Once he fired, there was nothing to hide behind. The rotunda was the worst place to launch a counter-attack. Something the invaders were most certainly already aware of. He glanced back over his shoulder. Jon's chiseled jaw was set. He nodded to Xander. There were two more men that had followed. Their guns were ready.

The screams dulled as Xander brought up his weapon. All the outside noise fell into some invisible distance as his eyes narrowed on the first man in his sights. There were only a few of the gunmen whose attention was on Xander's side of the room. All the rest were zoned in on the newly appointed president who was being escorted to safety. Xander's only job in that second was to give the men moving the president away as much help as he could.

It was time to be a problem.

Xander lined a man up and shot twice. As he moved the nose of his pistol slightly to the right, he saw blood spatter from the first man's neck. His next two bullets already entered the man beside the bloody one, and then two more hit a third gunman in the line. The sound of the men behind Xander firing their weapons made him flinch. That's why he missed the fourth gunman he'd aimed at with his first two shots. He corrected his aim, fired for the man's chest, and dropped him. A couple other gunmen fell beside the ones Xander was shooting. His men were doing their part.

It was like shooting fish in a barrel. The problem was, it was the same way for the gunmen. The rotunda wasn't a massive room. With nothing to hide behind, civilians were definitely taking fire. As Xander dove to the floor to dodge some return fire, Natalie flooded his mind. There was an almost magnetic pull to turn back to get her. Like a mother's instinct when her child is in danger. Not giving in to that feeling was like denying his own existence. As he fired his Glock until it was empty, not going to her was slowly breaking him.

Xander's Glock locked back. He ejected the spent magazine and quickly grabbed his spare from the slot in his shoulder holster, and slapped it into place. Just as soon as he racked the slide, he had to fire. There were a couple of men who had turned his way. Jon had just shot the one in front, keeping him from firing at Xander. They were making a dent on this side of the rotunda, but there were too many gunmen on the president's side of the room. They were losing the battle.

"Secure the doorway!" Xander shouted behind him. "Don't let any more in! They have to funnel down the hall!"

Jon looked back and motioned for the two men behind him to do what Xander asked. If they could keep more men from entering, Xander knew he could have a real chance at stopping the rest who were inside. The only question being, what damage would already be done?

Xander fired on a couple of gunmen who had turned their attention to the men Xander had sent to secure the doorway. He and Jon were successful at keeping them from being shot. Xander had made it to the first group of men that he had taken down. He took a knee, holstered his Glock, and pulled the sling of an M4 from around one of the dead gunmen's necks. He stuffed both spare, thirty-round magazines he saw in the vicinity into his pants pockets. Then he ripped off his suit jacket. The sounds of screams and gunfire were still echoing. There would be dozens dead by the time this was over.

Jon scavenged an M4 of his own. Now the two of them could do some real damage. The gunmen that were left had no idea Xander and Jon were coming up from behind. They were focused forward. It was clear that their objective was to leave the United States without a commander-in-chief. Xander looked at Jon and gave him a nod. Then he was off.

Xander jumped the downed men as he placed the M4's sling around his neck. As he moved forward and put the butt of the gun to his right shoulder and stared down the sights as he tried to find the next man he could take down. Most of the commotion in the room was at the opposite side of the rotunda. People were still trampling each other to get away from the bullets. There was shouting over by the door, but Xander couldn't tell what, or who it was. Then gunfire erupted from the hallway behind them where he'd sent his other two men.

"He's there! Shoot!" a man shouted in front of Xander.

The words echoed in between gunshots. Xander's stomach sank as he pressed forward. Somewhere, deep down, he knew whoever shouted that meant the president. Xander found a man aiming into the crowd and fired at him. A few other men turned when they heard Xander's M4. He and Jon took a knee and fired until they all dropped. Xander saw a man turn out of the corner of his eye. His gun turned straight toward Jon. Xander dove and hit Jon at his shoulders. They both rolled back and the man re-aimed at them. Xander pulled his weapon into position but watched as the man about to shoot dropped to the ground. One of the men from the hallway had doubled back and shot the gunmen before he could fire at Xander and Jon.

Chaos followed.

Screams—even louder and more terrified than before—erupted from the doorway everyone was trying to escape through. Men turned and fired at the man who'd just saved Xander. He and Jon returned fire. They dropped, but not before they took down their ally. Xander pulled Jon to his feet and they ran forward. He couldn't see any more gunman. What he saw down by the doorway was a group of people huddled, looking down over someone. A few women were sobbing.

Xander had to stay focused. In his mind, he knew who they were huddled over, but he had to make sure the room was being secured. He found two men in suits on the outside of the huddle. He recognized them from the security briefing. They were Secret Service. He yanked one of them back by the shoulder.

"Secure the hallway! Make sure no one else gets in! Take him with you!"

Both men moved without hesitation. Xander pushed forward through the huddle. When he got to the center and looked down, it was a sight he wouldn't forget for the rest of his life. He couldn't believe his eyes. It felt as though he were in the middle of a movie. Instead, reality had once again outdone fiction, and the worst had happened.

The president of the United States was dead.

CHAPTER FOUR

FOR THE MOMENT, THE SHOOTING IN THE ROTUNDA WAS over. They'd managed to put down all the men who had entered. However, it wasn't before the worst could happen. Chaos still filled the room. Xander finally pulled his eyes from the president's bloodied body on the ground and looked around. People were still screaming as they found more dead around them. They were still running over people to try to find safety. Xander knew they needed to get everyone in order as quickly as they could. Xander felt a squeeze on his arm.

"Is it over?" Jon said.

Xander turned toward him. "We have to act like this is just the beginning."

"You don't think that's true, do you?"

"I don't know what to think about what's happening. All I know now is that you are the president of the United States. And you need to get to safety."

The look on Jon's face brought Xander no comfort.

"X, I can't run to safety. Other than you, I'm the most trained here to be in this situation. I can't leave you now."

Xander looked around again, taking a second to think. Jon was right. But he knew all protocol ever written about the president was that he needed to be protected. At the same time, whoever wrote those rules had never seen a Navy SEAL in the Oval Office.

Xander gave Jon a nod. "Okay. But you have to stay with me. Like we're attached. No bullshit."

"Lead the way."

Xander looked around and found a chair. He walked over and stood on it. Before he said anything, he took a quick look where Natalie had been. His eyes searched the faces of the crowd. But he couldn't find her.

"Hey!" he shouted at the top of his lungs. This was not his strong suit, no matter how many times Sam had called him a loudmouth.

Jon walked over, stuck two fingers in his mouth, and did a massive wolf whistle that echoed through the rotunda.

"Listen up! Let me have your attention, now!"

Jon whistled again, and finally the crowd began turning their attention toward Xander.

"I know you're scared, but we can't panic!" Xander shouted. He looked to his right, beyond the huddle around the dead president. He saw Sasha, Jon's chief of staff, standing there ready for direction. He pointed to her. "Sasha! Can you find a chair and stand on it please?"

Xander gave her a moment. He watched her do as he asked. Then he pointed to her again.

"Follow Sasha to the House Chamber. The doors are bulletproof. We'll get you there where you will be safe while we figure this out."

"What the hell is going on out there?" a woman shouted.

Xander couldn't see her, so he spoke to everyone. "We will get answers! But for now, get yourself to safety."

"Is the president dead?" a man's voice shouted.

"Get to safety! Let's move!" He looked over at Sasha. When he gave her a nod, she hopped off her chair and moved to the doorway behind her.

"Follow me!" she shouted on her way. "This way! Let's go!"

"If you are uninjured, help someone who is!" Xander shouted. "As soon as we can, we will get medical personnel. I'm sure there is a doctor or two here. When you get to the House Chamber, medical people, please help tend to the wounded!"

Xander was about to jump down from his chair, but he couldn't. Not yet.

"Natalie!" he couldn't help himself any longer. He had to know that she was okay. "Natalie come to me if you can hear me!"

He searched the crowd that began to move in a wave toward Sasha. He didn't see Natalie. A pit was rapidly forming in his stomach. He would never forgive himself if something happened to her.

The murmuring began again in the crowd. The sobbing reignited as people were pulled from their loved ones who had already been killed. There was still no sign of his fiancée. Xander looked back toward the hallway where the men were stationed, looking out for anyone else who might be coming. Then he looked over at Jon. It occurred to Xander in that moment that he wasn't just looking at his friend, or even the vice president. Jonathan Vickers was now the president of the United States.

Xander looked back toward the crowd. When he did, gunfire erupted behind him. There were more men coming from the entryway. He needed to get Jon to safety. He jumped off the chair and grabbed Jon by the arm. He yanked him in the direction of the second doorway that led to the House Chamber. Jon turned and yanked his arm free.

"Our men are taking fire! We can't leave them!"

Xander looked him dead in the eye. "My priority is keeping the president of the United States alive."

Jon wore the shock on his face for a moment. Xander could see that he hadn't yet computed the chain of command after seeing the president dead on the floor.

"We don't have time to ponder it," Xander said. "Let's go!"

This time, Jon didn't pull against Xander's grip on his arm. Xander grabbed the only Secret Service man left that he could see and pulled him along. "Jon is the president now!" he shouted to the buzzcut man in the black suit. "Help me keep him safe!"

The people had pretty much emptied out into the next hallway toward the House Chamber now. Xander looked back one last time, hoping to see his woman's beautiful face. That's when he felt someone latch onto him from the side. He could smell her perfume before he even turned to see her.

"Xander!" she shouted in his ear as she wrapped her arms around him. "What's going on? What is this? The president is dead? Who would do this?"

Natalie was panicking.

Xander lifted her off her feet and carried her along with him, the secret service guard, and Jon. "Let me worry about that, darlin'. Let's get you to safety. We'll get this figured out."

The four of them came to the spot where the president was lying, dead. There was no way Xander was going to leave the body of a president out in the open for whoever was attacking them to take. God only knew what they might use his body for if they got their hands on it. At minimum, they would use it to claim whatever victory they were fighting for. That wasn't going to happen on Xander's watch.

Xander put Natalie on her feet. "Stay close."

She nodded.

He turned to the guys. "Jon, and you, help me with him!"

Gunfire was still echoing through the rotunda. It was getting closer. The men guarding the hallway weren't going to be able to hold them off for much longer. Jon and the Secret Service man lifted the president and hoisted him over Xander's shoulder. The now former president was much bigger in political stature than physical frame, so it was easy for Xander to hold him.

"Grab as many guns as you can, then let's go! I've got the president. Let's move!"

The four of them were the last to make it to the doorway. As they moved into the hallway, Xander took one last look back over the rotunda. One last look at the nightmare that people would be talking about for the rest of time. It looked like a war zone in that beautiful room. That's when it occurred to him that is exactly what it was. The United States was at war. That much was clear. What wasn't clear? Who was the enemy?

For the moment, that would remain unknown.

One of the men Xander had sent to the hallway came running back into the rotunda. Several gunshots rang out and the man fell face-first onto the floor.

Whoever the enemy was, they were taking no prisoners. They were killing anyone and everyone who was in their path. Including the president. Xander's mentality needed to shift into the same mode. All the battles, all the missions, all the death-defying acts, all culminated into this moment. It was time to be the man he'd been training to be for over fifteen years.

It was time to become the war machine.

CHAPTER FIVE

Xander began running as fast as he could with the president's body thrown over his shoulder.

"Move!" he shouted as he hurried through the National Statuary Hall.

The thought occurred to him how grateful he was that he had attended the security brief earlier. The only way he knew where he was going was because they went over a map of the entire Capitol Building, pointing out key things like the bulletproof doors installed in the Hall of the House of Representatives. Though Xander knew those doors wouldn't hold under what was coming at that moment. The only way all the people who were still alive were going to survive was if they could stop the insurgents before they made it to the House Chamber doors.

However, as he ran with what was left of the stragglers who were trying to survive, he realized there was nowhere near enough men left to stop anyone. Firepower wasn't going to help them survive; he was going to have to outsmart the enemy. That, and hope there weren't many more of them left.

Dotted along the hall there were battery-powered emergency lights glowing a white light. Without those, it would be difficult to see. It was surreal watching Natalie run for her life in front of him. Nothing, no matter what a man has been through, can prepare him for seeing sheer terror on a loved one's face. Xander was scared. Any man would be. But people like Natalie who had never known war, he couldn't imagine what it felt like. That's when his mind flashed to Paris. Eight years ago. He couldn't believe how time had flown as he moved through the final hallway to the House Chamber.

Akram Khatib. The man who had kidnapped Natalie and killed Xander's horse, King's Ransom. He felt like this terrible memory had come back to him in that moment for two reasons. One, to show him that Natalie had been through something horrific, and she not only survived, but thrived afterward. She could handle this too. He needed to stop worrying about her, and worry about saving as many of these people as he could. The second thing the memory reminded him of was just how outmatched he was in Paris. The odds were near zero of finding Natalie before Khatib killed her. But he and his team made it happen. He could make this happen too. He just needed to regroup and start going on offense. Playing defense was getting everyone killed.

The major missing piece, however, was his team. He currently had none of them. Kyle Hamilton, Dbie Johnson, and Samantha Harrison were all in DC. They were doing CIA business while Xander and Natalie were doing the inauguration thing. They were all supposed to meet up at the big after-party in a couple of hours. Now he had no idea if they were alive.

"What are we going to do now?" Jon shouted as they ran down the hall.

Xander shook from his thoughts as they ran toward the open doors of the House Chamber. The gunfire had ceased behind them. Xander knew that only meant the bad guys had no one left to shoot.

"We get everyone inside, then we regroup. See who we have left to fight."

"Xander, there is no one left," Jon said.

Xander didn't respond. He just nodded forward to the open doors in front of them. The words, HOUSE OF REPRESENTATIVES, in gold block letters above them. Then there was one more set of doors a couple of feet inside of that. Two men were standing there, along with Jon's chief of staff, Sasha, ushering people inside.

Xander followed Natalie and Jon inside. He walked the president's body over to his left, behind the first row of seats in the chamber. As gently as he could, he lowered the president to the ground. Then he turned to Sasha.

"Cover him up. Don't let people gawk at him."

She nodded and removed her blazer to begin doing what Xander asked. Xander stood and glanced over the room. There were maybe thirty people left. They were mostly huddled together at the podium in the far center of the chamber. The two men at the door came walking over with Jon. The same battery-powered emergency lights allowed everyone to see. It also gave the situation an even more ominous tone.

"They have training," Jon said. "I already gave them a weapon."

The two of them held up their M4s that were taken off the men in the rotunda. Xander looked over at Natalie. She still had a handful of rifles herself. He grabbed three of them, and left her with one.

"Keep that one for yourself."

"Xander, I don't—"

Natalie stopped talking when she saw his face. This wasn't the moment for conversation. Xander walked back over to the center aisle and first looked back out the doors. There was nothing coming down the hall. Yet. Then he turned toward the people at the podium.

"Anyone with any combat experience, or training, we need you now. I have two rifles left. If you know how to shoot one, it might be the difference in making it out alive."

A dark-haired woman stepped forward. She was unassuming in her long skirt and navy-blue blazer. "I can shoot. No combat experience, but my father was a Marine. He's been teaching me weapons since I was a kid. I'll do what I can."

Xander held out the rifle as she jogged forward. "Thank you." Then he looked around. "Anyone else?"

No one stepped forward. Xander ejected the magazines from the last two rifles and stuffed them in his pockets. It was probably better this way. Better that he had the ammo to shoot than someone who didn't really know what they were doing.

"All right, listen up!" Xander said as he turned to the people at the podium. "We only have one shot at this. Jon Vickers is now the president of the United States. Follow any orders he gives you. He knows what he's doing. I don't have any idea how many gunmen are coming for us right now. I'm not going to lie to you. So just cover up, say your prayers, and hope we can fight our way out of this. Whatever you do, no matter what happens, don't get in our way."

One of the men went to shut the first set of doors.

"Don't!" Xander said.

"What?" someone shouted from the podium. "What are you doing? Shut the doors!"

Xander didn't have time to explain. So he just addressed the man at the doors. "We are all dead if you shut those doors."

Jon walked over.

Someone else shouted from the podium. "What good does it do to have bulletproof doors if you don't close them! You're going to get us all killed!"

Jon stepped in front of Xander. "What are you thinking?"

"If they get to the doors, it's too late. We have a choke point in the hallway out there. If they want to be in here, they have no choice but to come through there." Xander nodded out the doors.

Jon looked out toward the hallway, then to Xander. He nodded. "It's our best chance."

Xander replaced the magazine in his M4. "Mr. President, it's our only chance."

CHAPTER SIX

Xander walked away from Jon and found Natalie. She was staring aimlessly out the doors toward the hallway, waiting with bated breath for death to come running around the corner.

"Natalie, it's time to focus."

She looked at him, but her stare remained blank.

Xander reached forward and lifted up the sling on the M4 she was holding. He moved it up and over her head. "You remember what I taught you?"

A few years ago, after what happened in Paris, Natalie said she wanted to learn some self-defense. Xander started her on some hand-to-hand combat, then some jiu-jitsu, then they progressed into weapons. Over the years, every few weeks, they would go and practice. Everything from knives to handguns, and even rifles. Natalie had fired hundreds of rounds through various AR-15s, M4s, and more. She had grown into a pretty good shot.

"I—I can't shoot this," Natalie finally spoke up.

"You absolutely can."

Natalie looked down at the weapon. Then back to

Xander. She looked worried. Xander knew she needed some baby steps.

"Give me a press check," he told her.

She looked down at the weapon again. It looked big in her arms. Her navy blue dress was torn at the shoulder. She still looked beautiful.

"Don't think about it," Xander said. "Just do it. Like you've done it dozens of times." Xander reached forward and tilted her head up at the chin to look him in the eyes. "You've been through worse. We will get through this together."

That seemed to help. The fog lifted from her eyes and she took the rifle in both hands. She first ejected the magazine, checked that it was full, then slid it back in place. Then she pulled the charging handle to load a round and released it. Xander gave her a smile.

"See? You're ready. But only shoot the bad guys, okay?"

Natalie didn't return his smile. But she was ready. He noticed her finger was resting outside the trigger guard, just like he'd taught her.

"You are last line, okay?" he said. "Let us do the shooting. Only if we get overrun do you help, got it?"

"Got it."

Xander stepped forward and kissed her on the lips. "I love you."

"I love you, too," she said.

"They'll have to kill me to get to you, you understand?"

She nodded.

Xander tried humor once more. It was his defense mechanism. He smiled. "And, I'm not sure if you know this or not, but I am really hard to kill."

Natalie didn't smile. "Be even harder to kill this time, would you?"

A fire lit in Xander and it was burning all the way to his fingertips.

"Xander!" Jon shouted. "I hear them coming!"

There was a chorus of screams from behind the podium. Xander ran toward the door. He sidled up on the left side, half his body hidden by the doorframe. The other half was waiting with his rifle ready to fire at first sight.

Like a tidal wave of armed men rolling down the hallway, they came. The eruption of gunfire was so loud that Xander's eyes were forced shut just to withstand the sting. He fired anyway, shooting right into the mass of gunmen running their way. Whoever was behind this invasion, this was them making sure the president was dead. And everyone else in sight while they were at it.

Xander could feel the bullets flying by. He got as low as he could to the ground and held his finger down on the trigger. He moved the muzzle of his rifle left and right, hoping to catch as many men as he could. After his first thirty-round magazine was spent, he got his first good look at who was coming. They were carrying riot shields. Offset behind them were the men who were firing. Xander ejected his mag, pulled a fresh one from his pocket, and locked it in place. He loaded a round then shouted before he fired.

"Aim low! They have shields! Aim low!"

He did as he'd told the others and aimed for feet. Just as he pulled the trigger, several rounds crashed into the doorway right beside him. He was forced to jump back. Xander dropped to his stomach to get lower, rolled, then fired as soon as his rifle made it around the doorway. Lowering the return fire was working. Men were starting to drop, but it wasn't fast enough. The mob of armed men was closing in. The only thing they could do to help their chances once it became close combat was thin the herd.

"Don't stop shooting!" Xander shouted. "Take out as many as you can before they reach us! Then be ready to fight!"

Xander knew that shooting bullets at oncoming enemies was a whole lot different than hand-to-hand combat. While it was Xander's specialty, he knew the rest of the people trying to help would be out of commission in seconds. As he fired the last of his second magazine, all he could do was hope that the wave of gunmen wasn't any deeper than he could see. Otherwise, none of them were going to make it out alive.

CHAPTER SEVEN

BERNARD CONLEY POURED COFFEE INTO HIS PORCELAIN-white mug from his French press. The rich aroma filled the room. Steam wafted from the cup as he set the coffee maker down. He'd used just about the last of the hot water in his estimation. Though the electricity was out, and would be for quite some time, his large office, filled with shelves of books and expensive artwork, had plenty of light. The oversized windows that overlooked Washington, D.C. let in an abundance of sunlight.

The calm in his office was a direct dichotomy to what was going on just a few blocks away. Though this particular room was quiet, he could still hear the gunfire roaring through the streets that surrounded the Capitol Building. Since cell service was also down, he wasn't able to get regular updates; in fact, thus far, he'd only received one. That the president had been shot. Whether or not he was dead was still unclear. However, Bernard wasn't worried. Without a way to get word to the military, and without a way for the military to get to the Capitol Building, he knew the waves of men he'd cast upon the city would be too much to keep the president alive.

Too much to keep anyone he wished dead—alive.

Three decades of planning had finally been put into action. No one thought he could pull it off. All of the enemies of the United States scoffed at the idea that Bernard could actually make it happen. Well, everyone but the Chinese and the Russians. And thanks to the open border policy of the previous administration in the U.S., Bernard had been building an army of his own for the last four years. The previous president's border policy was no coincidence. Bernard and his global group of friends had put the former president in the highest office in the land for this very reason.

Bernard walked over to the couch in front of one of the large windows. When he looked out over Washington, it looked different to him. Most likely because he knew it was never going to be the same. America was never going to be the same. And it was about damn time.

He took a sip of his coffee. He thought about how odd it was to not be able to check in with his men. Technology had rendered the entire human race impatient. A small price to pay for such a big day. He would get the good word soon enough. Then phase two could begin.

In the meantime, his global partners would really be chomping at the bit for their own update. He wasn't worried about them. They weren't the ones that had real skin in the game. But Bernard certainly couldn't have pulled off such a massive movement without them.

There was a knock at the door.

"Come in," Bernard said.

The door pushed open and another key player in the day's festivities walked in. Susan Dixon. The former Speaker of the House of Representatives, and still California state representative, moved inside. She was looking a bit haggard in her purple pantsuit. She was eighty-five after all. But maybe actually going through with all these plans was wearing on her.

"Hello, Susan," he said. His voice was rough and deep. "I just made some coffee. Pour some if you'd like."

"Thank you, but I'm okay." Susan's voice had a shake in it. She walked over and took a seat beside Bernard, but she didn't say anything.

"What is it, Susan? You should be wearing a smile, not a look of worry. We've made world history today. And after the next week, we'll likely be able to rewrite the history books as we see fit."

Susan's face formed a sheepish grin. "Yes, well, that is good news. But I'm sure there are several major hurdles we'll have to clear before that victory is claimed."

Bernard sipped his coffee and nodded. "Yes. No one said taking over the most powerful government in the world would be easy. But it's going exactly according to plan."

"So far as you know," Susan said. "We can't even check in with anyone. How do we know the military isn't forming at this very moment? There were plans in place for all of this."

"Yes, Susan. There were. And we put them in place. And we have the people in place to make sure what we want to happen, happens."

"And what *happens* when just one of them decides that all of this is too much?"

"You know," Bernard smiled. "Worry isn't good for fine lines." He nodded toward her forehead.

"I don't give a shit about *fine lines*!" she said as she stood. "I care about our families living through this. About them having us free, and not in a cell for the rest of our lives."

Bernard remained calm. "You knew the risks. If this is too much for you, Susan, you know you can get out at any time. Just don't expect any favors as we move into power."

Susan put her hands on her hips. Then she took a deep

breath. It seemed she realized her worry was only upsetting Bernard. "I'm just . . ."

"Nervous," he said as he wrapped his hands around his coffee cup and crossed his legs. "I understand. But infecting everyone here with your worry serves no good purpose."

"I suppose you're right."

"I will update you when I have new information. Until then, trust that our plan is working. We were meticulous with the details."

"I understand, but there are always variables. Kinks. Don't you think there will be someone, or something that puts a wrinkle in our plans?"

"Honestly? No. We have all the right people in all the right places. Not a single wild card that we've been made aware of. This nation is going to be ours, Susan. And its citizens will have no choice but to trust the ones who save them from this . . . invasion." Bernard pointed between himself and Susan. "Us."

Susan let out a sigh. "All right."

"Now go infect someone else with your anxiety. It's not going to grow in here."

Susan nodded and left the room. Bernard took a long breath and let it out to clear her presence from his own aura.

"The plan will work," he said aloud. "It will work."

CHAPTER EIGHT

XANDER INSERTED THE LAST MAGAZINE HE HAD INTO THE M4. It wasn't going to be enough to keep the men coming toward them down the hallway of the Capitol Building from breaching the door. For a moment he thought of closing it. But his instinct told him that it would not only just delay the inevitable, but possibly even give them time to get more soldiers to the House Chamber where Xander and the rest of the people inside would be sitting ducks without any more ammunition to fight them off.

They had to make their stand now, and recover more weaponry from the fallen men in the hallway. No matter how many lives it cost to make that happen. He knew it was the only way.

The air around him had an acrid, sharp scent of sulfur. He could feel a bead of sweat streaking down his temple. His heart was thudding. Not from the action, but from the impending doom. All of his life he'd been the man to save people. Now he faced his toughest challenge, made even harder knowing the love of his life would die with him if he failed.

As he rolled over, he glanced behind him. Natalie was ducked behind a row of seats, holding a rifle to her shoulder. She was brave. He was proud of her for not cowering in an impossible situation.

He had to get them out of this.

Xander aimed low and fired. To his right, he watched Jon's bolt lock back. He didn't reach for another magazine. He was out of ammo. Jon dropped the rifle and pulled a pistol from the inside of his suit jacket. It was just about over. One way or another. They had slowed the men coming down the hall, but they hadn't stopped them. They were just a few feet from them now.

Xander fired until his M4 matched Jon's—empty. One woman's scream set off a chorus of them. The people Xander was protecting knew the gunfight was over. They were going to have to fight, or die. As Xander jumped to his feet and reached for his pistol, a man with a riot shield plowed into him. He grabbed the top of the man's shield as he backpedaled. He yanked down, pulled the man to the ground. The man slid on his back, just about even with Natalie who was still crouched behind a seat.

The man started to get up, but Xander had already pulled his pistol. He fired once and the bullet burrowed into the man's forehead. Natalie screamed when his blood splattered her like a Jackson Pollock painting. Xander found her eyes and said one word. "Run."

She bolted out from behind the seat toward the podium at the back of the room as Xander spun and shot the first man he saw. As he dropped, another running at him raised his shield. Xander fired low, hitting a kneecap. He dropped his shield as he hit the floor and Xander put one in his head. All the men were masked. They had black neck gaiters pulled up over their mouths and noses. The dark goggles hid their eyes. However, it was clear to Xander that most of the men were not American. Their short stature and yellow-tinted skin clued him in. Had the Chinese actually invaded?

Before he could ponder, he saw Jon and the men around him get overrun. Xander ran forward, glancing to the hallway. There were still more men coming, but he could finally see the end of them. Maybe twenty more. If they could just survive this last wave, maybe they could make it.

As he approached the scrum where Jon was now on his back, bullets splintered off the wooden outside railing of the row beside Xander. He dove to the floor, popped up to a knee, and fired the last seven rounds in his Glock. He dropped it as he pulled his Benchmade Claymore knife from his pocket and pressed the button to release the blade. He reached forward and pulled the man on top of Jon toward him as he jammed the blade into his throat. Blood ran like a waterfall as they both fell backward. Xander was covered.

He shucked the man to the side and rolled as a gunman fired at him. One of the other men fighting with Xander shot the gunman twice before he could move his gunfire to the right. As he fell, Xander caught the end of his rifle with his free hand and yanked it from around the man's body, but before he could turn the gun around to use it, he was run over by another man and his shield. Xander's feet left the ground and he landed hard on his back. He lost the gun but maintained his grip on the knife. The shielded man's momentum put him on top of Xander. Xander reached around the shield and plunged his blade into the side of the man's neck.

Xander pushed the man from on top of him, keeping his shield. As he stood, through the bloodied shield, he watched the man who'd just saved him take several bullets to the chest. Xander charged forward and knocked the shooter off his feet. Jon finished him off with a couple of rounds from his pistol he'd regained after being taken down.

Xander's ears were ringing. The shield was slippery in his hands from the blood. His eyes were wide as he tried to find his next target. He didn't have to look far. Three more men were on top of him and they'd shielded their way right through Jon's defensive gunfire. Xander dug his feet into the floor and pushed forward, but the impact of two men was too much. Once again he was knocked off his feet. This time, he lost the knife in an effort to keep the shield he was holding as a barrier between him and the two men.

It was no use.

One man was yanking on the shield and another had already started throwing punches. Xander managed to jerk his head to the side, avoiding one punch, and then taking the second one in the shoulder. With his left hand, he pulled toward him on the shield, and when the other man pulled back, Xander let go. The man tumbled backward. This allowed Xander to get both hands on the man punching him. He dug his left thumb into the man's eye, caving it backward into his skull. The man screamed as Xander used his thumb grip to slam the man's head into the wooden rail beside him.

Xander did a technical stand, keeping his head away from the man coming at him that he had pushed away a second ago. The man no longer had his riot shield. Xander wasted no time and threw an overhand right that smacked into the man's temple. He stumbled back, and then blood splattered from his chest. Xander whipped his head around and saw Natalie aiming her rifle. There was no time to let it sink in. Jon had just been slammed to the ground by two more men. Three more were running in behind them.

Xander took two power steps forward and fired his hips. The top of his foot hit the man punching down on Jon in the forehead. The smack was audible. He fell to the ground, unconscious. As the other three men came running up, they were met by the last two Secret Service men that were left.

Xander looked down and stomped on the neck of the man he'd just knocked out so he wouldn't be getting back up.

Jon was handling the man who was fighting him. Xander bent down and took the rifle from the man he'd just stomped. As he turned it in his hands, gunshots echoed through the House Chamber. Xander looked up and the two Secret Service men were lying on the ground. He'd brought the rifle up as he reacted to the gunfire and laid on the trigger, moving the rifle left and right, until the last three men were down. When they'd all dropped, Xander was still firing. He felt a hand on his forearm. It was Jon. Jon gave him a nod and Xander let the trigger go.

Above the ringing in his ears, he could barely hear some women crying behind him. The room was absolute carnage. Bullet holes in everything that wasn't covered in fallen bodies. It was nothing short of a massacre. But they'd somehow survived it.

Xander turned to find Natalie. She was looking at him, but her eyes were blank. She was somewhere inside her own head. Probably hiding herself from the current reality.

"You okay?" Jon said. His voice was muffled. Xander's ears had yet to recover.

Xander nodded. "You?"

"Still here. What the hell do we do now, X?"

Xander finally let himself exhale. Then he shifted his brain back into survival mode.

"I don't really know," he said. "But we can't stay here."

Xander knelt down beside one of the several dead men lying at his feet. He pulled their goggles off and pulled down the black gator covering the man's face. He was Asian.

"The Chinese finally made their move," Jon said.

Xander stood. "Can't be just them."

"No, it cannot. Russians?"

"Possibly. But to coordinate something like this on American soil . . ." Xander didn't know how to finish that sentence. He didn't want to say Americans were involved. He didn't have to.

"Americans had to have a hand in it."

Xander nodded.

"What are we going to do now?" a woman shouted from behind the large wooden podium at the back of the room. Her voice was shaking. Terrified.

Xander was about to answer when he noticed Natalie's head whip to the left in the direction of the hallway. Her mouth dropped open. Xander spun to look behind him. At the far end of the hallway, coming from the doorway that led to the Capitol's entrance, men came flooding in. They were dressed exactly as the men they had just defeated. Another wave was coming.

There was no way they would be able to survive this one.

CHAPTER NINE

XANDER DOVE DOWN TO THE GROUND TO PICK UP ONE OF the dead men's rifles that lay at his feet. As he pulled it up to aim it down the hallway, he shouted, "Incoming! Fire everything you've got down the hallway!"

As Xander began to fire, Jon started shooting beside him. There were only two other men with guns. There was no way it would be enough. But Xander knew he wasn't going to stop fighting until the bitter end. All he could do was hope that they would spare the people behind him. Most importantly, he prayed they would spare Natalie.

Soldiers streamed into the hallway. There were so many that Xander couldn't help but further lose hope. He swallowed his emotion as he fired into the crowd of gunmen coming their way. He and Jon both hit the ground as return fire came back at them. Xander kept firing with one hand as he turned and waved for Natalie to get down. He watched her dive behind the wooden tables before turning his head back to his fate.

One more of the Secret Service men dropped as his blood showered the surrounding area. Xander took more than a few drops of it. His magazine was empty. He dropped the rifle and grabbed the one lying on his left. He pointed it toward the hallway and once again started firing. But he only got three rounds out of it before it, too, was empty. He didn't see another gun close enough to reach without getting up. And as soon as he did that, he would be a dead man.

Xander heard Jon's rifle click empty. They shared a doom-filled glance.

It was over.

The final Secret Service man that was trying to help them shoot their way out of this mess was hit when he moved for a rifle that had some ammunition left. The only reason Jon and Xander weren't being hit was because of the droves of dead bodies piled in front of them. The men were moving methodically down the hallway. They weren't in a hurry. They knew they had it won.

Silence roared in the House Chamber. The ringing in Xander's ears was the only sound he heard. It was like watching a movie with the volume off as the men moved toward him. The difference was, this horror show was real. He wanted to go back and hold Natalie, but he wasn't going to quit. No matter how imminent death was, he would fight until the end.

The men were halfway down the hallway. Xander could see that they were still aiming their weapons in front of them. Waiting for someone to make a move. If someone did, they were dead. Xander was going to wait until they were on top of him to make his move. He was going to try to take as many of them with him to death as he could. He didn't suppose he would get too many before they shot him.

Xander let his head fall. His only shot at any sort of violent retaliation was the element of surprise. If they thought he was dead, he could maybe get a couple of them with his knife. However, his body jolted when he once again heard the sound of gunfire. He immediately recognized, though, that it wasn't coming from the men closest to him in the hallway. It would have been louder. This gunfire was farther away. Almost as if it were coming from behind the men in the hallway.

Xander jerked his head up for a quick look. He found that the men who were almost at the chamber door had turned their backs to him. Someone had surprised them from behind. There was no time to waste if he wanted to take advantage of the moment. His adrenaline spiked as he jumped up and moved on all fours like a gorilla to snatch a rifle lying on the ground. As soon as he had it in hand he did a front roll into the aisle where he had cover from behind the wooden rails.

As he raised his weapon he saw Jon get up out of the corner of his eye. A spark of hope lit within him as he aimed and held the trigger. He moved the rifle left and right as the rounds exploded in a continuous burst. The men in the hallway were dropping like flies. So much so that Xander stood and stepped out from behind the wooden rail. He then stepped over the dead men in the aisle. As the magazine in his rifle went dry, he bent over and picked up another from the floor. There was no shortage of ammunition. He sprayed the men in front of him as he moved toward the door. He took cover just behind the doorway. Jon's gunfire stopped as the last of the men fell under the onslaught.

Xander peeked around the doorframe. There was movement, but it was a long hall, and whoever was on the other side was being cautious like Xander. Staying back out of the hallway. Jon had moved up and was standing just on the other side of the doorway. He put two fingers to his eyes. Xander shook his head, letting him know he did not have eyes on the shooters. The people they were protecting were growing restless behind him. They were worried who was at the other end of the building.

Xander's ears were still ringing, but he was finally beginning to hear the silence that was all around them now. It was just Jon and Xander left with any combat experience now. If this wasn't help at the other end of the hall, they were all dead. His breathing was still rapid, but it was starting to regulate. He glanced back and saw Natalie poking her head out from behind the podium. He didn't know how long it would last, but he was glad they were both still breathing.

Xander waited. Both sides were being overly cautious. Neither one of them wanted to make a mistake. He knew he needed to get the people still alive out of the building, but he wasn't going to rush this. Not now. So, he just kept his grip on his rifle and stayed ready. But he was running out of patience.

Just when Xander thought about doing something to see what awaited them at the far end of the hallway, he heard someone whistle. Two sharp tweets came echoing down the hallway. Xander was almost overcome with emotion.

It was Sam.

CHAPTER TEN

WHEN THE SOUND OF SAM'S WHISTLE MADE IT TO THE House Chamber, Xander took a sharp inhale and smiled. They had just bought a little longer to live inside the chaos that had descended upon Washington, D.C. He stepped out from behind the doorway and peered down the hall.

"Sam?"

"Xander!"

Xander squinted his eyes as something moved at the end of the hallway. Then, in the white light of the emergency lights, he noticed someone running toward him. "Xander!"

Xander's feet began moving before he realized it. His heart pounding. Two more people came running around the corner behind her. "Sam!" He was at a jog now.

"X!" he heard Kyle's voice echo. It was like a song to his ears.

"Kyle!"

They were all running now. The last figure that had moved into the hallway was noticeably larger. Xander hadn't spent a lot of time with the man, but the one thing you couldn't forget was just how large of a man was Lawson

Raines. Sam didn't slow down as she got to Xander. Instead, she jumped into his arms, nearly knocking him over.

"Holy shit, Sam," Xander said as he squeezed her. "You all saved our ass!"

Kyle hit the two of them with a hug and the three of them stumbled backward.

"We thought you were dead!" Kyle said.

Xander managed to fit him in the hug. "I thought we were, too."

The large shadow with them came walking up. "We should stop meeting like this."

Xander let go of Sam and Kyle, and looked up. "Lawson Raines." Xander clapped his hand around the lunchbox-sized hand that was reaching toward him. "I couldn't agree more."

Lawson pulled him into a man-hug. Xander patted him on the shoulder. Natalie had run up and she was getting her hugs in with Sam and Kyle.

"Lawson, this is my fiancée, Natalie Rockwell."

Natalie walked over and held out her hand.

"I'm well aware," Lawson laughed. "My daughter is a big fan. She keeps me up on all the gossip."

"Thank you for coming to help us," Natalie said as she shook his hand.

Lawson looked over at Xander. "What the hell is going on?"

Xander stepped back so he could see all four of them. "I was hoping you all had more information?"

Kyle shrugged. "Big explosion. Lights went out. Sam said we needed to come here to find you. That's literally all we know except for the sheer chaos outside."

"We nearly died on more than one occasion," Sam said. "It's a full-on war out there."

Xander couldn't believe it. The day had started out so normal. A beautiful day, at that. Now the history books were being rewritten with every passing minute. "What's it look like out there?"

"Soldiers everywhere," Lawson said. "EMP, then shooting. They were ready. This entire thing was years in the making."

"How bad is it here?" Sam said.

Xander glanced over at Natalie just in time to see reality wash over her. He looked back at Sam. "It's worst-case."

"How worst-case?" Kyle said.

"The president is dead."

Sam gasped. Xander understood. It's only happened a couple of times in the history of the United States.

"Holy shit," Lawson said.

"Yeah," Xander said. There were no other words.

They all stood in silence for a moment.

Xander looked at Sam. "You remember Jon Vickers?"

"Not outside of the news of him becoming vice president and that he's the one that brought you here. You served with him, right?"

"I did. He's alive. And he's now the commander in chief."

"Thank God for that," Kyle said.

"There are about twenty more inside the House Chamber. Some former presidents, dignitaries, and so on. None of them will survive without us."

"And how are we going to survive?" Lawson said.

Xander looked at him. He could feel the seriousness of the question. With that, Xander knew that the three of them hadn't exaggerated how bad it was outside of the Capitol Building. The fact that they had risked everything to come to him and Natalie was such a massive gesture. Especially for Lawson. He had a daughter. Unfortunately, he had no answer as to how they would survive. He did, however, know the way forward.

"One step at a time."

Lawson nodded. He knew there really wasn't any other

response. "I'm the guy who normally just says the stuff everyone is thinking. So, shall I start now?"

Xander nodded. Everyone turned their attention to Lawson.

"There are really two pieces to this. I'm not advocating anything, just laying out facts. There's our survival." He pointed at everyone standing in their circle. Xander, Natalie, Kyle, Sam, and himself. "And then there is everyone's survival. Those two things are very different."

Xander understood exactly what Lawson meant, and why he said it. Natalie did not.

"You mean, there is everyone's survival, and nothing else," Natalie said.

Lawson held up both hands to say don't shoot the messenger.

Sam spoke up. "Yes, Natalie. In a perfect world, there is everyone's survival and nothing else. What Lawson means by what he is saying is that we are now at war. Literal war. The rules don't work the same now."

Natalie's face scrunched. "I don't understand what that means. There are twenty or so people in there who need you all to live. You're suggesting we just leave them behind?"

"No, Natalie," Xander said. "That isn't what Lawson and Sam are saying—"

"It sure as hell sounds like it!"

"It's not. Please listen. We don't have time to talk out everything. Lawson is simply bringing up all the information so that we can have it all out on the table. The five of us here have a much higher chance of surviving today if we are on our own. That doesn't mean that's the call we are making, but what Sam is saying, in war, these are the conversations that need to be had. Then we make the call."

"That sounds like a lot of words just to say who is important enough to save and who isn't."

"Sometimes that's what it comes down to, Natalie. If we don't survive, we don't have a chance to stop what's going on out there. That's the call. It's not about who's important enough to live, it's about us living so that we can try to save a whole lot more than twenty people."

Natalie started crying. "You think the five of us can stop this? No communication? No soldiers? No anything!"

Xander pulled her close. "Sam and I have been the people to stop this sort of thing for over a decade. I have no idea what we can do. But there are soldiers, Natalie. They are mobilizing as we speak. I know it feels like we are alone here, but we aren't. Our soldiers will fight until there is nothing left to fight for. We just have to survive long enough to meet up with them and fight this together."

"I don't mean to be insensitive," Kyle said, "but we have to start making moves."

Natalie pulled away. "Maybe I should go see if I can help anyone who might be hurt."

"I think that's a good idea," Xander said.

Natalie walked away. She was trying to dry her tears.

"Sorry, X," Lawson said. "I should have waited."

"Don't be sorry. We'd be dead if it wasn't for you guys. Let's make a plan and start executing. Before we get executed."

As the five of them walked back toward the House Chamber, Xander couldn't help but feel worried. As he thought about the word, worried, he laughed to himself. Worried was just about the most understated way to describe the feeling of impending doom that weighed on his shoulders. He could talk a big game to the others about a *plan*, and executing a plan, but there was no next move. There was no CIA consult. No Dbie just a phone call away to gather intel. Hell, at the moment, they couldn't even look out the window to see what was going on.

According to Sam, it wouldn't much matter if there was a window. Apparently, it was a war zone outside. While Xander was used to war zones, he always came well-equipped, and armed with knowledge. He had neither one of those things at the moment. But he knew he needed to snap the hell out of Negativetown. It would serve no purpose to stew on the things that weren't.

Xander looked to his left. Lawson's massive frame loomed over Sam, and even Kyle, who would never be described as small. No matter how bad things were, they were better with them by his side. The four of them together could give much larger groups of men a whole lot of trouble. That was probably the ultimate plan. Wreak as much havoc on the enemy as they could until they fell. And if they fall, at least they'll be together. He couldn't help but be thankful for that.

Xander looked to his right. Natalie. The love he thought he'd never find, being who he is, and his given profession. Yet, there she was. As gorgeous as a sunset over the ocean, and just as fiery. She sure had sparked a flame in him. And here she was, one of the few to survive the massacre that just happened. He had to be thankful for that too.

They were in the worst situation he'd ever been in. But things could still be worse. He didn't just have his country to fight for. He had his loved ones to fight alongside. Whoever the enemy turned out to be was going to have an awfully hard time keeping Xander from keeping them alive.

If nothing else, he was going to make sure of that.

CHAPTER ELEVEN

"WHAT THE HELL ARE WE GOING TO DO NOW?"

Xander and crew had just walked back into the House Chamber when a man walked straight toward Xander. It was surreal for Xander as he looked the man in his blue eyes. He'd seen him on television dozens of times. President Bush was in office when 9/11 happened. This wasn't the way Xander envisioned meeting the man.

"You got crammed back here in this death room. What the hell are we going to do now that we're backed into a corner?"

Xander looked down at the white-haired man. It's funny how reality can humble your perception of someone. Of course Xander knew that President Bush was not a large man, but in person, he seemed much smaller. Not just in stature, but in aura.

"Mr. President," Sam stepped in, "all due respect, but you're alive aren't you?"

"Well, yeah, but—"

"It's okay, Sam," Xander said. "I'm sure he's grateful. But now he's scared. I don't blame him." Xander looked back to

President Bush. "Mr. President, I don't have time to explain anything to you right now, but I assure you, my only focus is getting all of us out of here alive." He looked right to Natalie. "This is my fiancée." Then he looked to his left. "And these are my best friends on the planet. No one wants to see everyone live more than I do."

President Bush swallowed hard. "I meant no disrespect. I just know the president is dead, so someone needs to lead these people."

Jon Vickers walked up.

"There's your leader, Mr. President. Jon here is our president now. He's in charge."

Jon smiled, but then nodded back to Xander. "Not on this mission I'm not. He'll be the man steering this ship."

"You sure, Jon?" President Bush said. "You have combat experience."

"Not like Xander."

President Bush looked back at Xander, but his expression changed. "Xander? As in, Alexander King?"

"Yes, sir." Xander was surprised the former president knew of him.

"Well, hell, why didn't you say so? Everyone involved in Washington knows who the hell you are and what you've done for this country. Apologies. I'll let you all get down to it." He reached out his hand.

Xander gave it a firm shake. "Yes, sir. We're going to give it all we've got."

"Then we are in good hands here from what I know."

President Bush turned and walked away. Xander noticed he had a slight limp. Then all thoughts of former and sitting presidents were gone. It was time to face what had come for them.

Xander walked down one of the rows of chairs to put

some distance between him and everyone else. He waved his team over. "What exactly does it look like outside?"

Sam put her hands on her hips. "Worse than you've been imagining."

Xander looked at Kyle. Kyle nodded and then let his head fall.

"Okay. Let's have some details. How'd you get here? What did you see? How long do we have in here? Anything."

"I assure you we don't have long," Sam said. "We came from the Hyatt Regency a few blocks away. Normally about a fifteen-minute walk or so. It was chaos. So it took a lot longer. We were having lunch next door when we heard a massive explosion. Then the power went out. Obviously, the first thing we did was check our phones. My heart dropped when the three of us had no service on two different cell carriers."

"That's when I noticed none of the cars were moving out on the street," Kyle said. "It was the strangest thing I've ever seen. Full stop. People getting out of their cars, trying to figure out what the hell was going on. That's when Lawson said, 'EMP'."

Xander looked at Lawson.

"It was the only thing that made sense," Lawson said. "Then the gunfire started. That's when we knew we had to find you, X. We had just been talking about how the inauguration was going on, and how bored you must have been."

Xander laughed.

Lawson continued, "It's a good thing they moved it into the Capitol Building."

"Not sure it could have been much worse," Xander said. "The president is still dead. Fear of an assassination attempt was the exact reason they moved it inside."

The four of them were quiet for a moment. Then Sam picked up the story.

"Lawson had to bust our hotel door down to get to our weapons. Then we took the back way here. Let's just say, that wasn't uneventful. There were more than a couple of times where we almost didn't make it."

"They were just executing people in the streets," Kyle said. "Who's doing this, X? Any idea?"

"Judging by some of the dead gunmen they sent in, I've seen a mix of Asian and Caucasian. So, could be China, Russia, and probably a lot of American mercenaries."

Kyle shook his head but didn't say anything.

"Let's focus forward," Xander said. "What's our move? Is it better to stay here? We have no shortage of weapons."

Lawson said, "Do you think whoever is doing this knows the president's dead?"

"You think that makes a difference?" Kyle said.

"Don't know. No idea what their goal with this was. I'm assuming something on this scale is an attempt at a full-scale takeover, right?" Lawson looked at Xander.

"I've been having the same thoughts. If this is as well coordinated as it seems, and we haven't seen any of our military show up, they must have crippled them first."

"You mean, hit them before the EMP?" Sam said.

"Or at the same time."

"So, then what are we going to be able to do?" Kyle said. "Our only objective should be to survive, right? Without communication, there is no way we can fight this."

Xander was quiet. Kyle was right. Where they were at in this entire thing lent very little in the way of fighting back. He had the sinking suspicion mere survival was going to be just as tricky. However, Xander didn't know what not fighting back meant. Fighting back was surviving in his line of work. It's the only thing he knew. Though he had no idea what that meant for them in that moment, it was still the only way forward. To fight. It was the only way to survive.

CHAPTER TWELVE

BERNARD PEERED OUT HIS OFFICE WINDOW. WASHINGTON, D.C., was in disarray. He could see his men moving through the streets. Spreading the word that everyone must stay inside their homes. He knew that wouldn't last. Once food or drink became low, people would start to panic. That would be phase two. Chaos control. Or, better said, controlled chaos. He and his group would have to let people get some of their worry out of their system. Then he would roll out plans for food sharing and regain their trust. Then the sheep would slowly start to follow the shepherd's orders.

"Mr. Conley?" a woman's voice from the door.

Bernard turned to find his assistant. "Yes, Marcy?"

"Jackson Bale is here to see you."

Bernard perked immediately. His number one soldier had returned with an update. He could feel his heart skip a beat.

"Yes, please, send him in."

Bernard turned his back to the window as he watched Marcy walk out the door. He wasn't nervous, but what Jax had to say meant a lot to the movement. If things were going well early, it would be much easier to keep them moving in the right direction. And the president being dead, along with his second in command, would go a long way to easing a transition of power. The people would expect change at that point. Fewer questions would be asked.

He tapped his fingers against his forearm as he stood with his arms folded across his chest. Waiting. A deep inhale came next. Then a slow exhale. Finally, the mountain of a man that was Jax Bale walked through the door. Jax was a tight end in the NFL before an injury ended his career in his third season. That was fifteen years ago. Ever since, he put the same training regimen and discipline to use as being a weapon for the US Military.

Bernard first heard about Jax when he killed half a village just outside of Baghdad. He was immediately thrown in prison for his actions. The reason Jax was working for Bernard and his globalist group now was because Jax believed he did everything he was supposed to do on the mission, but the United States instead made him the scapegoat. Jax gave his all for America and she turned on him. That sort of scorn never really goes away. It fueled Jax to see things Bernard's way. The way that the US and its global partners needed to be changed. Forever.

"Jax, good to see you. How is it out there?"

Jax took a few steps toward Bernard. His six-foot, six-inch, two-hundred and thirty-pound frame made the room look smaller. The sunlight from the windows bounced off the dark skin of his bald head, and shone off the sweat that glazed his massive, chiseled arms. He looked like a menace in his black t-shirt and black pants. All covered in combat gear from shoulders to toes.

"So far so good."

Bernard could hear the slight southern drawl in his voice from Jax's Texan roots.

"Is he dead?" Bernard cut to the chase.

Jax hesitated.

Bernard's stomach dropped.

Jax stepped closer. "There was more resistance at the Capitol Building than expected."

Now Bernard stepped forward. "What the hell does that mean?"

"It means that there was more to the men than you told me were going to be in the president's security detail. One of my men who made it out said that someone near the president was moving like a trained operator—*special* operator, not a Secret Service agent."

"So is he dead or not, Jax?"

"He went down. Whether he survived or not, I don't know yet."

Bernard shook his head. He couldn't believe it. He couldn't help but hear Susan's voice asking him about how there is always a problem. He wasn't happy that she was right. He looked up at Jax. "So, why don't we know? Didn't I give you like thirty men to get this done?"

"You did. Apparently, whoever this operator was, he was able to push them back with the help of the president's men. Including Vice President Vickers."

Bernard began to pace. "So, the only two people outside of the designated survivor who can technically run this country might still be alive? Even though I made sure they were both in the same location, took out the entire country's power grid, and served them up on a silver platter for you—who is *supposed* to be this super soldier—and you can't confirm that either one of them is dead?"

"I was coordinating the securing of the designated survivor, sir."

Bernard laughed. "They let you get by with excuses like this in the military?"

Jax just stared ahead.

"Why the hell weren't you in that building making sure these two were dead?"

Jax cleared his throat. "It was a mistake. One I won't make again."

"So you're going back in there and making sure it's done?"

"I am. But it will take me away from running point on securing the White House."

"I need full control, Jax."

"I can do both. With the grid down, and no military able to roll in, I can get it done."

"You better," Bernard said. "If you don't, we all go down. You understand this?"

Jax nodded.

"This is the difference between actually changing the United States of America, or dying in it. You can be that change, Jax. No more pointless wars. We will control the entire world."

Jax was getting ready to speak when the two of them heard a noise from the back of the room.

Bernard cocked his head and looked at Jax. "Was that a . . . a sneeze?"

Jax looked over his shoulder. "Did it come from the office beside us?"

Then they heard it again. This time, it was clearly a sneeze, and it wasn't coming from any other office but the one they were in.

Jax turned to face the noise. Bernard took a step toward the cabinets at the back of the room. With a crash, the bottom cabinet door flung open and a young man dove out onto the floor. Bernard and Jax were so caught off guard that they just stood and watched as shaggy-haired teenage boy jumped up to his feet. He was holding his hands out in front of him.

"I'm sorry!" the boy said, his eyes wide. "I didn't hear anything. I didn't mean to be in here!"

Then the boy bolted for the door. Bernard's synapses fired as his mind caught up. The boy had heard everything. "Get him!"

The boy slammed the office door behind him as he ran. Jax rushed the door and whipped it open. Then he charged down the hallway. Bernard jogged to the open door and shouted down the hall. "Don't let him out of here!" He watched as the boy opened the door to the stairwell and disappeared. Bernard felt himself tense as he watched. Then he took a long, calming breath as Jax entered the stairwell after him.

Bernard let worry fade. Jax would catch the boy. However, even if he didn't, what did it matter? Everyone who he could run and tell was already under Bernard's thumb. The entire US defense system was, in fact. So, he turned back inside his office, traded his coffee cup for a whiskey glass, and went to grab a bottle to sip from as he awaited Jax's confirmation about the death of the president and vice president of the United States of America.

Then it was time for phase two.

CHAPTER THIRTEEN

Xander slammed a full magazine into another of the fallen enemy's rifle. He then handed it to Natalie. She took it and threw the sling over her head. Xander had a rifle over his shoulder, and had stuffed six magazines in his pants. Sam had done the same. The rest of the team was explaining to the civilians in the House Chamber what was happening. Or, for them, what wasn't happening.

"I don't like this," Jonathan Vickers said to Xander.

Xander secured one of the magazines that was loose in his belt line. "What's the alternative, Jon?"

"Me going with you," he said. "I'm the only one here other than Sam with your kind of Special Operator training. You need me."

Xander squared up and looked him in the eye. "Jon, like it or not, you are the President of the United States now. That changes things."

"No, it doesn't."

"Yes it does!" Xander raised his voice. He looked around and cleared his throat. Then he softened his tone. "Yes, it does. We don't know what they have planned out there. But we can assume that some of the rest of our politicians are compromised. It's the only way something like this could get coordinated. Right?"

"Okay, but so what?" Jon said. "If you and Sam don't survive, we are in *real* trouble."

Xander sighed. "I hate to break it to you, but we're already in *real* trouble. And, it matters what happens to you. If the next in line for president if you die is compromised, there won't be much to stop them from doing whatever they want. Maybe there isn't already, but we have to keep some semblance of our republic. We need information, and we need it now. All of you stay here, doors shut, ready to fight if someone comes for you. We're going to go get the lay of the land."

"I don't like it," Jon said.

"I don't care," Xander said.

They stared at each other for a moment. Then Jon finally cracked a smile. "That's no way to talk to your Commander in Chief."

They both laughed. Jon stepped in and gave Xander a hug. When he backed away, he was still smiling. "Ever thought about being a politician? I could use a vice president right now."

"I have enough people wanting me dead. Why raise that to half the country?"

"You sound like my wife, who, thank God, had to stay home with our newborn."

"See, we have a little luck going for us," Xander said.

"Find some more while you're out there, would you?"

"Do my best," Xander said. Then he looked over to Sam. "You ready?"

"Ready."

Xander turned and gave Natalie a long embrace.

"Be careful," she whispered in his ear.

Xander leaned back. "I prefer being dangerous."

She leaned in and kissed him. "I love you."

"I love you."

Xander turned and looked at Lawson. Kyle had just come walking up. "You guys keep these people safe. We'll be back soon."

Lawson nodded. "Keep your focus out there. We're fine in here."

"Yeah, we're good," Kyle said. "Stay sharp."

They turned and looked at Sam. Kyle smiled. "Keep him safe, would you?"

Sam laughed. "Been my job for many years now."

Without further ado, Xander nodded to Sam and they both started for the door. "Lock up behind us. I'll tap the door with the butt of my rifle three times, pause, then two times when we come back."

"We'll be here," Kyle said.

Xander and Sam walked through the House Chamber doorway. Xander looked down the hallway at all the dead men strewn about. He watched as Sam stepped over one man as if he were a stone.

"How the hell did we get here?" Xander said.

Sam glanced over. "Is this an existential question, X? Or literal, as in how'd we get stuck in this building with all these dead people?"

Xander looked around. Thought for a second. "I meant it existentially, but it actually pertains to both."

"Well, existentially speaking, we've been over this ad nauseam. This is who we are, we don't know any other way, blah blah blah. You really still doing this?"

Xander was quiet for a moment as they wove their way down the hall toward impending doom.

"I guess since being back with Natalie, now getting

married, it's weighing on me more. I mean, next thing up for us is that we have a kid, right? That's the natural order."

"I suppose that is the order of the civilians."

"But how the hell do I keep doing this if I am a dad? I don't want to be out here with my life hanging by a thread with little Johnny or Susie at home."

Sam laughed. "You've already named them, have you?"

"You know what I mean, Sam."

"I don't much like serious Xander. I prefer you snarking at me as we go into battle."

They were coming up on the turn toward the rotunda.

"Never mind."

Sam sighed. "All right, if you're going to pout—"

"I'm not pouting," Xander snapped.

They stopped at the edge of the hall, poked their heads around the corner, and found the coast to be clear. They made the right turn. The sea of bodies stopped for a while.

Sam picked up the conversation. "Shall I be honest?"

"Do you know any other way?"

Sam stopped in her tracks and turned to face Xander. "If we're being realistic, we're not making it out of this."

Xander's stomach dropped. He was not used to Sam giving up before the fight was even half over.

Sam continued. "This is different, Xander. If only one of us is lucky enough to survive, it will be considered a win. It's clear this has been well planned a long time ago. There is no sign of our own soldiers, and there are plenty around the D.C. area. That means they were taken offline at the same time the EMP hit. If not before. Probably bombs in place that all went off together. They probably took out bridges. They probably secured generals and other high-ranking military commanders. And they are probably regrouping to make another—bigger—surge into here to make sure the people who'd been transferred power here today had no capacity whatsoever to help retain that power."

"Then why not just blow up this building?" Xander said.

"It was moved late, remember? Too much security and cameras around this building to do anything last-minute."

Xander shook his head. "So, what you're saying is, stop worrying about the future, because you and I don't have one?"

Sam shrugged her shoulders. "You see it another way?"

Xander looked back at the carnage in the hall behind them. Then thought of all the dead bodies waiting in the rotunda. Who knows how many outside. No way to communicate with anyone outside the building. No getaway vehicles. At the moment, he did not see another way out. But he wasn't about to tell her that. One negative mind was bad enough. Two was suicide.

Instead of answering, he let out a sigh and walked forward.

"Yeah, me either," Sam said.

CHAPTER FOURTEEN

"What's the goal here, X?" Sam said.

The two of them were almost to the front entrance of the Capitol Building.

"Get the lay of the land, I guess."

"All right. So, do we shoot if we see soldiers in the distance, or is this just recon?"

"I don't know, Sam. Let's just feel it out."

They were quiet for the rest of the walk. The rotunda looked like a scene straight out of a horror movie. The tile was painted red with blood. Bodies on top of bodies. Some the good guys, some the bad guys, but all of them dead. The small, windowless hallway leading out to the east entrance showed no sign of the disaster inside. Their footfalls echoed off the smooth, pale sandstone blocks.

Xander stopped short of the seventeen-foot, bronze, east entrance doors. He could almost peek out through the seam that ran down the middle. He could feel the cold penetrating the historic doors. He touched the bronze bar on the door as he looked at Sam.

"We ready for this?"

"No," Sam said. "But we are the people for the job."

Xander nodded and pushed open the door a couple of inches. It was heavy, and it creaked as it gave way. The cold and the sunlight rushed in. The afternoon had given way to early evening, but the sun was still strong. A steep flight of stairs swept down to the plaza, dotted with flags snapping in the breeze. He poked his head out a little further. Manicured lawns stretched out toward the Supreme Court and the Library of Congress. Usually there would be traffic humming from Independence Avenue. But not that afternoon.

"Anything?" Sam whispered.

"Nothing. It's like the city is frozen."

Xander scanned the wide portico platform. There were a few fallen Secret Service men lying on the concrete. Outside of that, just a few statues lurking in the shadows. He stepped through the cracked door for a better look. Beyond the Capitol grounds he could see some people moving like ants, but they didn't look like soldiers in formation.

He scanned left. In the distance, black smoke billowed toward the deep blue sky in a few different spots. Then he heard gunfire. It wasn't close, but it was a lot. He ducked back inside.

"Nothing close that I can see. But there is shooting."

"What are they doing?" Sam said. "Just killing everyone in sight? Taking out police or anyone who might be fighting back?"

Xander nodded. "Probably anyone with a badge and a gun."

"This is insanity." Sam paused for a minute, listening to the gunfire rattle. "Okay, so it's clear for now at the entrance. So what? You and I could escape, run the streets, probably get away. But the twenty or so people in the House Chamber can't."

Xander shook his head. "I don't know what to do, Sam.

We can't help them escape, but we can't help this situation if we just stay here and try to protect them. Eventually, we're going to run out of ammo."

Sam put her hand on her hip. "All we can do is lead them here, or to the west entrance around the back if it's clear. Arm them. Let them run for their lives. Only then will we be able to make progress on this situation, if that is what you're wanting to do."

"What do you mean if that is what I am wanting to do?"

"There is an army of enemies here in DC right now, Xander," Sam said. "We would need an army to fight them." Sam sarcastically looked in all directions around her. "In case you haven't noticed, we don't have one of those. What would you have us do? The president is dead. The city is locked down by some tyrant who clearly has been planning this for quite some time. There are only a handful of us, with no resources, and no way to contact anyone for information."

Xander clenched his jaw. "Then we find the tyrant. Do what we do, Sam. Cut off the head of the snake!"

Now it was Sam who shook her head. "Okay, X, and how do we find this tyrant? There is no Dbie to call to investigate. We have zero intel. No direction at all. Are you understanding that we are completely without our normal mission-based tools? Like, all of them?"

"I understand everything completely. But we still have us." Xander pointed between the two of them. "We've pulled off some fairly crazy shit in our day. Things that everyone outside of us would have said were impossible, Sam. But we did it. We won. And we can win this!"

"Xander, I appreciate all of that. But this . . . this is different. It's completely different and you know it!"

Xander didn't like it. But he did know it. He knew she was right. Of all the monumental tasks he and Sam had resolved, this was much bigger. Much more . . . hopeless. The word stung him as it crossed his mind. However, before he could talk any more with Sam, more gunfire rang out. But this time, it was close. Inside the building close. And the bewildered look on Sam's face as she flinched sent an ice-cold chill down Xander's spine.

"Natalie!"

CHAPTER FIFTEEN

XANDER SPRINTED DOWN THE HALLWAY, THROUGH THE rotunda, and into the next hallway. The House Chamber wasn't far now, yet he felt miles away. Now he could hear screams echoing alongside the rattle of gunfire. His mind showed him violent images of Natalie lying in her own blood. He shook them from his consciousness and pulled the rifle strap to secure the gun in his hands. Sam was right on his heels.

When Xander turned the final corner, the chamber came into view at the end of the hall. Only one of the large doors was open, but it had men trying to pile inside. Xander slowed as he turned to motion to Sam. He pointed at the small pile of four bodies up ahead on the right. He didn't wait for her to respond. He dove forward and slid along the floor until he was right behind the pile.

As Xander moved his gun into firing position, he felt Sam slide in beside him. He opened fire on the men trying to get into the room filled with his people. After a couple of them dropped, some of the men began turning their fire toward Xander and Sam. He stayed low and continued to shoot. He sprayed until the charging handle on his M4 locked back. He ejected the magazine with his left hand as he pulled a fresh one from his right pants pocket. He slammed it into place, pulled the charging handle, and continued firing.

The bodies in front of him and Sam were just enough to block the bullets coming their way. As a couple of the men tried to move closer to get a better angle, Xander and Sam made sure they couldn't. The line of men was thinning. As Xander kept shooting, he knew it was time to set the people inside that room off on their own. The gunmen were just going to keep coming until a report was sent back to whoever was in charge that everyone in the Capitol Building was dead.

Xander could see that Kyle and Lawson were able to stop the men that had reached the interior of the chamber because Lawson had just come into view. Xander rose to a knee and motioned to Lawson by pointing to Lawson's right, letting him know that's where the men were coming from. Xander trained the end of his weapon on that side. He wasn't positive, but he was pretty sure that was the route to take to get to one of the back doors of the building. Made sense because that is where the men were coming from.

The hallway was quiet. He could hear himself and Sam breathing heavily. It was a tense moment. His heart rate was speeding. Xander watched as Lawson moved forward. He poked his head around the corner. He didn't raise his gun. Xander got to his feet and walked forward, keeping his rifle in ready position. Lawson stepped out into the hallway.

"We have to get the hell out of here," Lawson said, still staring down the barrel of his gun.

"We couldn't agree more," Xander said. "The front was clear a couple of minutes ago. I think we take everyone there and hope they find their way to safety."

Lawson lowered his gun and looked at Xander. "There's no other choice."

Xander turned to Sam. "Keep an eye out here while I round everyone up?"

Sam nodded. "Maybe make it quick?"

"Yep."

Xander nodded for Lawson to move inside. He then followed him in.

Lawson looked back over his shoulder. "Pretty sure we'd all be dead if you hadn't come back to help."

That's when Xander saw Natalie running toward him. She nearly knocked him over as she threw herself into him. Xander gave her a squeeze, but he was all business.

"Help me round everyone up. We have to get out of here."

"We are sitting ducks in here, soldier," former President Bush's voice rose above the murmurs.

Xander looked right and found his eyes. "Yes, sir. It's time to go."

President Bush turned to the people. "You heard the man. Let's get the hell out of here!"

Jon came walking up. "What did you see?"

"Pretty clear out the front exit. We just have to escort everyone there and try to keep them safe as they go out on their own."

"And the president's body?"

"I don't know, Jon. But I know we can't take him with us."

Xander turned away from Jon and addressed the room. "Everyone please move toward the door. We will escort you out the front. I suggest you grab a weapon on your way out. I wouldn't go out there without being armed."

"Then what?" a woman said. "We aren't soldiers! We can't fight them!"

Xander didn't see who spoke, but he still answered. "You can't stay in here. They are going to keep coming. Your best bet is to leave through the front door, and run for safety."

The people talked amongst themselves as they moved. Xander looked over at Natalie. "You're staying with me."

Natalie nodded.

"Let's go people!" Lawson shouted. "Everyone out! There could be more men coming as we speak. We have to go!"

Kyle walked over.

"Take the front with Sam," Xander said. "She knows where to go."

"What are we going to do?" Kyle said. "After we get them out?"

Xander just shook his head. "I don't know. Fight our way through D.C. until we find someone with some answers I guess."

Kyle nodded. "Whatever it takes. These bastards can't just overthrow the United States. Somebody has to stand and fight. Might as well be us."

Kyle walked away. The people were moving through the aisles toward the doors. Xander looked over and saw Jon standing over the president's body. He could see the emotion on Jon's face. However, he couldn't find words that would console him, so he turned for the door.

"Everyone follow Sam!" Lawson shouted. He was waving his arm, coaching people to keep it moving.

Xander walked out with a few of them. He couldn't help but feel like he was letting them down in some way. It felt wrong just to lead them to the exit, and then watch them walk off into such dangerous conditions. Sam caught his eye as he exited. She gave him the all is still clear nod. He walked in the direction that the men had last invaded from. All seemed quiet. He turned back and watched the people step around the bodies lying dead in the hallway. Some of them took the time to find a weapon, but most just kept walking.

Natalie was waiting by the door. She was pointing down the hallway for people to follow. Kyle was about halfway down the hallway in the front of the line. Xander made his way toward him so he could help Kyle navigate to the east entrance.

They were quiet as they walked. Kyle had been Xander's best friend since fifth grade. They'd done all of life together. Even the craziness of Xander's chosen work. It had actually pulled his friend into the same field. In that moment, Xander only thought of the good times. He didn't want what they were walking toward to enter his mind. He just let some of the good times they'd shared flow through his consciousness. Sports in school, chasing girls, even chasing the bad guys. They'd always had fun. He looked over at his friend, walking with his rifle in hand, and genuinely wondered if they would ever have fun again.

They'd made it through the rotunda and once again, the oversized bronze doors came into view down the hallway.

Kyle looked over at Xander. "So, we're just going to open the door for them, and wish them good luck?"

"I don't like it either," Xander said. Then he shrugged. "But we only have two choices. We either continue to babysit everyone here, keeping them alive, with no time for anything else, or we let them go, and maybe be the only viable crew that can make some sort of difference in saving a whole hell of a lot more people."

"Just doesn't seem fair."

"It never does. Yet we've made decisions like this our entire career. I don't know about you, but I want to find whoever did this. We can't do that with twenty-some civilians tagging along. Surely you don't think it would be safer for them to go running toward danger with us, do you?"

Kyle was quiet as Xander began pushing open the door.

He looked back at Kyle. "Do you?"

"No. Definitely not. So, that's what we're doing then? Running toward danger?"

"Have we ever done anything else?"

Xander didn't need an answer. He nudged open the heavy door and took a look outside. The people he was trying to set free began crowding into the hallway. He heard Sam asking them to keep it down. Things outside the building looked about the same as last time. Just a little less sunlight. The afternoon was fading. Also fading were the chances of making any sort of progress before nightfall.

Xander stepped back inside and looked at the people gathered in front of him. The light was low in the hallway. Probably better for him so he didn't have to see the fear on their faces in full light.

"If you don't have a weapon, my suggestion is to stay with someone who does. I'm not going to lie to you. It will be dangerous out there."

"You're going to stay with us, aren't you?" a woman said.

Xander didn't see who it was, so he addressed everyone. "We are going to go try to find who did this to our president, and to our country. We can't do that and keep you safe."

Murmurs began in the crowd. They were scared. Xander moved on.

"I suggest you get to cover as soon as you can once you step out these doors. And as much as I hate to say it . . ." Xander stepped forward away from the doors to make sure everyone could hear him. "I would consider anyone that you might encounter outside these walls as dangerous. Either steer clear of them, or be ready to fight. That's all I have."

Just then something slammed into the door behind Xander. Everyone with guns whipped around, ready to fire. Xander moved his gun to shoot. Just as his finger slid over the trigger, he pulled it back outside the trigger guard. In front of him, leaning against the massive, half-open door, was a teenage boy. Desperately sucking in breaths as he bent over at the knees, holding one hand out in front of him as if to say "don't shoot!"

No one moved.

"Are you okay?" Xander said.

The boy stayed doubled over. Still gasping for air. Xander gave him another couple of seconds as the crowd of people looked on.

"Let me know something, son," Xander said.

Finally, the boy lowered his hand and raised his head. He looked Xander right in the eye.

"They're coming."

CHAPTER SIXTEEN

BERNARD MADE THE DECISION, AFTER WATCHING JAX WALK out the door after the teenager that had been hiding in the cabinet that he was only going to worry about what he could control. It's how he got to where he was, and it was how he was going to finish the plan to change America forever.

The evening had settled in. The light outside his office windows was fading. He blew out the match he'd lit to spark a few of the candles he'd had ready around the room. Robert Patton should be arriving any minute. He would have some details of how things went on the West Coast. He had been communicating with them just before their EMPs shut out all the lights.

There was a knock at the door.

Bernard turned and watched the silver-haired, tall, fit man walk through the door. Rob had just turned fifty-five. Young for this sort of work. He reminded Bernard of himself about twenty years ago.

"Bernard, it seems like everything is going well here in DC?"

"Come on in, Rob. Things are just fine."

Rob walked over and gave Bernard's hand a firm shake.

"Any trouble making it over?" Bernard said.

"None at all. VW vans from the sixties might not have all the creature comforts, but they get the job done when the grid falls."

Bernard nodded. "True classics. How'd things go on the western front this afternoon?"

"I spoke to everyone just before the six launches. Everyone was in place and ready to execute. I have no reason to believe there were any hiccups." Rob tucked his hands down into his pants pockets. "More importantly, Bernie, how'd things go at the Capitol Building?"

While Rob was talking, Bernard had picked up his glass of whiskey. It was a good time to take a sip. He absolutely hated loose ends. Even more than that, he hated admitting they happened on his watch.

"I don't like the hesitation," Rob said. "There a problem?"

"No problem. Just lack of confirmation."

"On the president? Are you serious? What if he's on his way to the White House right now? How are you so calm?"

"Relax, Rob. There isn't a route from the Capitol Building to the White House that I don't have covered. Besides, he was reported as being shot. We just don't have his body. That's all."

"Well, why the hell not? Didn't you wipe that place out hours ago?"

"I just got documents back from the Secret Service meeting this morning. There were a couple of people at the inauguration that weren't supposed to be there."

Rob's face scrunched in confusion. Bernard knew how absurd it must have sounded.

"So? How does that stop *anything*?"

Bernard took another drink. "It won't. But this guy isn't just some ordinary citizen."

Rob shook his head and moved his hands to his hips.

"There is nothing to worry about," Bernard jumped back in. "Jax is headed down there right now to make sure everything is all tidied up."

Rob's demeanor softened. "Well, that does make me feel better."

"On top of that, we've still got our plant. Jax is going to make sure they are alive as well."

"Plant?" Rob said. Then it registered. "Oh, yeah. Well, everything should be fine then."

"It is just fine."

Bernard purposefully left out the part about the snooping teenager who was hiding in his office. If he thought it had an ounce of bearing on what was happening, he would have mentioned it. But it didn't.

"Let's move on to phase two, then," Rob said.

Bernard nodded. "My thoughts exactly."

"What's the timeframe?"

"We wait until Jax gets back with our asset. Then we can head over to the White House and begin setting everything up for tomorrow."

"How are we on defenses?"

"We're good. All the bases surrounding DC have been locked down. We'd been moving non-computer vehicles off all the bases over the last few months. We also replaced command over the last couple of years with our guys."

"So what does tomorrow look like?" Rob said.

"We will start bombing the major cities tomorrow. Teams have already been placing explosives throughout the afternoon. Once that starts, there won't be much for us to do but wait. Without the government on television and radio telling people what to do, there will be chaos."

"How long do we let that go?"

"I really don't think it will take longer than a few days,"

Bernard said. "Chaos will hit quickly. Especially as we spread word that we are under attack."

"Then, we just come in and save the day?"

"Exactly. We restore power. Then we *save* the American people. Laws will have to change in order to keep them safe going forward. Digital currency, the social credit system, it will all fall in line easily. The vast majority of Americans are sheep. COVID taught us that. Then we start to rebuild this country the way it should be. Under our rules. Under our *rule*."

Rob shrugged. "Won't be long before the rest of the world falls in line."

Bernard walked over to his bottle of whiskey and grabbed another glass. He poured as he spoke. "One world government. The way it should have always been. Decades of work, finally paying off."

He handed Rob the glass, then clinked his against it.

"To making history?" Rob said.

Bernard smiled. "To making the future."

CHAPTER SEVENTEEN

"THEY'RE COMING," THE KID SAID.

The look on the teenage boy's face was sheer terror.

"Who's coming?" Xander said.

"The bad guys. The real bad ones."

Xander knew that could be anyone under the rule of whoever was in charge. He reached forward and pulled the kid inside.

"How'd you know to come here?"

The wide-eyed boy stared at Xander.

"Talk to me, kid!" Xander said.

The boy shook his head as if erasing a trance. "I heard them talking about this building. They were worried about who was inside. Is that you? Can you help?"

Xander's gut churned. His mind raced through all the negativity of the last few hours and landed on the boy's words. "Who? Who was worried?"

Did they actually have a lead? Could this boy really know something?

The boy ripped his arm from Xander's grip. "They're

coming! They were right behind me! Please don't let the big guy get me!"

All of Xander's questions would have to wait. Kyle had just opened fire through the half-open door.

"Whoever he's talking about, they're here!" Kyle shouted.

Panic hit the crowd like a dropped glass—sharp, immediate, and impossible to ignore. Kyle dove back inside as return fire ricocheted off the bronze door. Xander glanced at the crowd and fear struck. He was surrounded by a waking nightmare. Citizens who had no idea how or when to use a gun, all armed, all scared to death. It was a disaster in the making.

Xander reached over and grabbed the boy, pulling him away from the door.

"Do not fire your weapons!" he shouted.

"Get out of the hallway!" Sam's voice rose above the crowd. "But do not fire!"

However, as soon as more rounds clanged against the door, people lost their composure in a rush. One woman began firing at the door. Bullets bounced around the hallway like hailstones ricocheting off a tin roof. Someone next to the woman grabbed her and took her to the ground.

"If you panic now, we're all dead!" Natalie shouted.

"Everybody back!" Xander shouted. He looked back at Sam who was standing beside Lawson. "We'll use the hallway as a choke point! Get them back!"

Kyle fired through the open door, hoping to keep the enemy back.

"Jon!" Xander shouted as he continued to pull the boy away from the door. "Take a couple of men and make sure no one comes up behind us!"

He then pushed the boy toward Natalie. "Get them back! Everyone get back!"

Natalie put her arm around the boy and began shouting

at everyone to move. He rushed forward for the door to pull it shut when a flash-bang clanged off the door and spun on the hallway floor before it exploded.

The flash didn't just shine—it revoked shadows, bleaching every corner white-hot. It left Xander's eyes ringing like struck bells, even after the bang had passed. All he could hear was a single metal note, pitched exactly between a scream and a migraine. It nearly knocked him over. He swam through the pain, disoriented, doing his best to find the door. It wasn't working. He couldn't pull his faculties together. Thankfully, someone pulled at him.

Xander still couldn't hear, but he let himself be led. He blinked over and over again, as if that would help wash the light from his eyes. Slowly as he was pulled, he could hear murmurs again. He began seeing shadows. He wiped at his eyes with his non-gun hand. Now he could see shapes. He could hear voices, though they sounded as if they were under water.

Then the gunfire rang clear.

So did the screams.

This time he felt someone shove him so hard that it threw him forward off his feet. He thought he heard a man grunt, but he couldn't tell if it was real, or if his mind was still clearing the fog.

Xander felt one more tug at his arm. It was so strong, he knew immediately that it had to be Lawson Raines pulling him.

"Stay down!"

Xander finally could make out the words Lawson was saying. All he could think of was Kyle. Kyle had been right beside him at the door when the flash bang bounced inside. The gunfire continued around them.

"Kyle!" Xander's voice sounded muffled, but his ears were recovering. "Get Kyle!"

"Stay down!" Lawson shouted again.

Xander ripped away from Lawson's grip. Though things were still blurry, he could see now. Lawson had pulled him from the hallway into the rotunda. He looked around. Behind him he saw Natalie and Sam ushering people deeper into the room. He saw former President Bush and others following. He watched Jon Vicker's chief of staff helping a woman back to her feet. Lawson was pulling at Xander's shirt, desperately trying to get him to take cover. Everyone was accounted for. Everyone except for his best friend in all the world.

"Kyle!" Xander shouted as he once again ripped away from Lawson's grip. He raised his rifle as he moved forward. The chaos around him dulled, like after the flash bang hit, but this time he was fully aware. The shouts of his name to stay out of the hallway muffled like he'd just placed noise-canceling headphones over his ears. He could see sparks ripping off the bronze door at the end of the hallway. He could see a few of the people he'd been trying to protect lying facedown on the marble floor.

The front end of a rifle showed itself at the door and Xander shot until the man carrying it dropped to the floor. Xander followed the man's body with his eyes until he landed flat on the floor.

That's when Xander saw Kyle.

He also saw a pool of blood.

Kyle was surrounded by it.

Sam went jogging by on Xander's left. Maybe she was shooting. Maybe she wasn't. He wouldn't know. The world around him had tumbled into a waking nightmare. The edges of his vision blurred. His heart thudded in his chest. Kyle was lying on his side, staring at the sandstone wall across from him.

Xander knew in an instant that his worried thought

earlier—the one where he wondered if he'd ever have fun with his friend again—had just been answered.

The answer was no.

CHAPTER EIGHTEEN

A FLOOD OF EMOTIONS IS SO CLICHÉ. HOWEVER, SOMETIMES things are said so often because they are universally true. Seeing his best friend in the world lying in his own blood came as close to the feeling of being completely overwhelmed as Alexander King had ever been. And he'd witnessed his parents being murdered right in front of his family home. Xander was as close as it gets for a human being to say they'd seen it all, and it not be a total lie.

But this was different.

This took his breath away, his heart away, and his will to go on from him in an instant. Then it came back on fire, and it lit every ounce of his being with a flame that he knew in that moment would never stop burning. Ever.

Xander ejected the magazine from his rifle, pulled a spare from his pocket, and slapped it in place. He pulled the charging handle and let it go. His rifle was ready to fire. He stepped over his friend and stalked toward the door. He felt Sam grip his arm as she shouted, "No, Xander!" He ripped his arm free and continued for the door. The only thing that kept repeating in his head at that point were the last words the teenage boy said before the shooting began.

Please don't let the big guy get me!

Xander was just in front of the door now. His mind was already hunting for *the big guy*, even though he wasn't even out the door.

"Xander, no!"

Natalie's voice rose above the fray. It was unmistakable to Xander.

"You can't just walk out there! Please stop!"

Xander didn't stop. He was already squeezing the trigger before he was all the way out the door. Several men came into view out on the East Front Plaza. They were all caught off guard by the crazy man shooting without cover. The first few went down with Xander's bullets, and the row behind them began retreating. A few of them turned to fire, but they were introduced to a second string of gunfire; Sam had made it outside. She wasn't going to let Xander self-destruct all on his own.

A few more of the men dropped. There were plenty more to shoot at. So Xander and Sam continued. Xander went until his magazine was spent. As he swapped for a fresh one, he called out who he was looking for.

"Where's the big man, huh? Where are you, you piece of shit! Show yourself!"

"Xander, let's get back inside!" Sam shouted. "Please! Kyle would not want this!"

Xander snapped his head to the right, staring in Sam's eyes. The orange glow of the setting sun faded behind her. "You saw him? You saw what they did to him!"

Sam fired a few times into the gunmen. "Not here, Xander! You'll get us all killed!"

Xander looked back toward the gunmen who were once again turning to fire. Everything around him was red. His brain had shut off normal operations. Something inside of him had snapped. He began firing.

"Where is the big man?" he shouted. "Come on!"

More shooting.

"Xander, please!" It was Natalie's voice behind him.

Xander turned and saw a man in all black standing behind her. His rifle was on the rise. It was too late for Xander to shout. It was too late for him to get his weapon in position to shoot. All he could do was scream.

"Natalie!"

Just as the muzzle of the man's rifle made it to the back of Natalie's head, a blur like a torn page ripping itself from a book streaked out of the door. The next thing Xander knew, the gunman was flying across the plaza, his heels above his head. Lawson Raines went skidding across the concrete. As if shooting a clay pigeon, Xander raised his rifle and sprayed the man with bullets before he hit the ground.

Sam was providing cover fire behind him, but they were out in the open. Xander turned to help her shoot as Lawson got back to his feet. Xander watched Sam nod toward Xander out of the corner of his eye. He felt the powerful grip of Lawson attach to his shoulders.

"No! Let me go!" Xander shouted.

He tried to pull away, but Lawson was too strong. He'd wrapped his arms up under Xander's armpits and was dragging him toward the door. Sam was shooting as she backpedaled.

"Let go of me!" Xander shouted again. It was no use. He was going to be pulled inside.

Just before he reached the threshold, a man taller than the rest of the gunmen on the far side of the plaza emerged. Xander raised his rifle to shoot, but his magazine was already empty. The two large men collapsed onto the marble floor of the hallway. Xander watched as Sam pulled the door shut.

Xander didn't get what he wanted. But he got something. He closed his eyes and let the image of the square-jawed, behemoth of a man that was staring right at him when he was pulled inside, burn into his consciousness. Burn was the exact right word too, because everything inside of Xander was on fire. He could feel his skin stinging with want for revenge. His blood bubbling beneath it. Boiling.

There wasn't a thing in the world that was going to stop Xander from finding that man again. He didn't care if he had to die trying.

At the moment, it didn't seem to matter. Because Xander felt as though the man he was at the start of that day was already gone. So he was going to take anyone he could down with him.

No matter what it took.

CHAPTER NINETEEN

XANDER STORMED INTO THE ROTUNDA. HIS MIND WAS racing a thousand miles a second. It was on revenge, then his friend, then keeping his fiancée safe, then back to revenge. He searched the ever-shrinking crowd of people for the boy who'd come running into the Capitol Building just a few minutes ago. He spotted him sitting on the marble, holding his knees, leaning back against the wall. His forehead was resting on his arms.

Xander jogged over and pulled the boy up by his arm. "Who the hell was that man?"

"Ouch, you're hurting my arm!"

Xander loosened his grip but didn't let go. "Who was he? Where did he come from?"

Xander was shouting.

"Xander!" Natalie shouted from across the room.

Xander didn't let up. "Who the hell was he kid? You led him right to us!"

"Xander! Let him go! Now!"

Xander dropped the boy's arm. Anger surged through

him like an electric current. He whipped his head around to look at Natalie. He was seething.

Natalie held up her hands. "It's not his fault. He was just trying to warn us."

"Yeah? And now Kyle is . . ."

A new wave crashed through his system. This was reality. For the first time, what happened in the hallway finally hit him. His demeanor changed. His shoulders slumped. And finally, his heart broke.

Emotion poured out of him in the form of uncontrollable tears as he collapsed to his knees. He couldn't breathe, it came at him so fast. Natalie slid to her knees and took Xander's head in her arms. She didn't speak. She didn't tell him it was all going to be okay. She couldn't, because she knew it wouldn't. He fell into her arms and nearly knocked her over. But she held strong.

"He died trying to save me," Xander wept. "He pushed me away from the bullets. I felt it. His last move was to make sure I was safe. But I'm supposed to be the one who does the saving!"

Natalie gave him the space to let it out. However, he didn't have anything left to say. His mind was a war zone, but the next thing that came to him was what Sam said out on the plaza. That Kyle wouldn't want this. Then the words he just spoke echoed, and he repeated them out loud. This time with less emotion, and more feeling. "I'm supposed to be the one who does the saving."

Xander rose to his feet. Natalie loosened her grip but didn't let go. The only thing Xander had left as wardrobe was a white tank top undershirt untucked from his pants. He lifted the shirt and dried his eyes. He took a long breath, let it out, then did it again. Then he looked into the eyes of the love of his life.

"I'm supposed to do the saving."

"It's okay, you can't save everyone. It's not your respon-sibility."

"You're right. I can't save everyone. Especially not Kyle. But I can save you from this God-forsaken situation. That's exactly what I'm going to do."

Xander turned back to the boy and stepped toward him. Natalie almost spoke, but she let Xander be. Xander looked back over his shoulder and saw Sam and Lawson standing guard at the hallway entrance.

The boy looked frightened as Xander walked over. "I'm sorry," he told the boy. The boy who couldn't have been much older than fifteen. "I didn't mean to scare you." Xander was calm now. The operator had stepped back into his body. The heartbroken friend was nowhere to be found. "You came to the right place. I'm the man they're worried about."

The boy brightened a bit. He stood upright and looked at Xander with something that seemed like hope.

"What's your name?" Xander said.

"Santi."

"All right, Santi, can you please tell me everything? Because there is a good chance that you coming here and finding me, might just save this city. Maybe more. But only if you tell me everything you know."

Santi nodded and gathered himself. "My mom is one of the cleaners at the Ford House Office Building. I was . . . well . . . somewhere I wasn't supposed to be this morning and I got stuck in some man's office. I think he's really important."

"Do you remember the man's name?" Xander had completely settled now. He was finding a rhythm in playing the part of the operator. The purpose of it all breathed a calm into his nervous system.

Santi shook his head.

"All right. What else? Did you hear something important?"

This time he nodded. "Yeah. I think so. Whoever he was, he's why all of this is happening."

Xander felt his fist involuntarily clench.

"At least that's the way he talked."

"Okay, good," Xander said. "What did he say that made you believe that?"

"Lots of things, but he was talking to the big guy I was asking you about. The first question he asked him was if the president was dead."

Xander saw Natalie take a step forward out of the corner of his eye. Like Xander, she couldn't believe what she was hearing.

Xander nodded. "Okay, good. Go on."

"That's . . . that's when the big guy—his name is Jax by the way—that's when he started talking about you."

"Jax. Okay, great. How do you know they were talking about me? And why were they?"

"Sorry, I just assumed it was you since you seem like the leader," Santi said. "The Jax guy said the report was that the president went down, but couldn't be confirmed dead. He said they couldn't confirm it because somebody who was more than just a Secret Service agent pushed them back. Said you were some sort of special operator or something."

"All right. Thank you, Santi. So, is that why you came here? You thought since I helped drive the men out of this building that I might be able to help?"

"Yes."

"And how is it that they ended up following you here?"

"They were coming here anyway," Santi said. "I sneezed where I was hiding and that Jax guy chased after me. I didn't want to lead them back to my house, so the only thing I could think to do was make it to the guy who ruined their plans and see if you could help. Help me, and all of us."

"I don't think I ruined anyone's plans. Yet. But I might

have slowed them down. Anything else you can tell me about the man who was talking to Jax?"

"He's been talking all day about planning this for years. I was hiding there for a long time. I think that's why he sent Jax after me. So I couldn't tell anybody what he was saying. Things like changing America, no military can help because there's no power, and something about a survivor? I wasn't sure what he meant. But secure the White House was in there. It was a lot. I'm sorry I can't remember it all."

Xander placed his hand on Santi's shoulder. "You did really good. You were really brave to come here. How long did it take?"

"Seemed like forever, but I'm not sure. I was so scared."

"I'm sure." Xander looked at Natalie as he paused for a minute. Then back to Santi. "If I get you back to the Ford House offices, you think you can lead me to this man's office?"

Santi's face dropped. Xander could see fear grip him.

"I—I can't go back there. There were so many men."

"You let me and my team worry about the men."

"Xander, I don't think Santi going out there is a good idea," Natalie said.

"You think staying here is?"

Natalie didn't answer.

Xander looked back at Santi. "Let me ask you this, Santi. Would you rather be here, or out there on your own? Or with me and a few people who have trained their entire lives to kill men like the one's you're telling me about."

"Well . . . when you put it that way . . ."

Lawson walked up from behind them and cleared his throat. Xander looked over at him.

"I realize this is a dumb question, but are you all right?"

Xander gave it real thought. So much so that he could see Lawson begin to feel awkward in the silence. "No. No, I'm not all right. The friend in me is hurting." Xander went quiet again for a few seconds.

"It's okay," Lawson said. "I'm just trying to see where we are and—"

"But I'm a compartmentalizer," Xander interrupted. He was looking down at the ground. "I learned it when my parents died." Xander looked back up at Lawson. "The operator in me will give me an escape for now. I'm good. Let's get down to business."

CHAPTER TWENTY

SAM AND LAWSON HAD BEEN KIND ENOUGH TO MOVE KYLE from the entrance. Xander knew he should probably say something to Sam. He felt she was probably having the same thoughts. Like a true brother and sister relationship, however, they knew what each other needed in the moment. That was to move on with business so they didn't have complete and total nervous breakdowns.

"What did the kid have to say?" Sam said.

"He knows where the office is of someone high up in this situation. He knows the name of the big man we saw outside who is running things for him from a military aspect. So, we need to make our way to the Ford House offices. The kid—Santi—knows where it is. After a little convincing, he said he'd take us. What about everyone else here?"

"We told them they were on their own," Sam said. "I think it was quite obvious by what just happened that we can't take care of them all." Sam nodded her head toward Natalie who was talking to Santi. "She going with us?"

"I'll die before I leave her behind now."

Sam nodded. Xander could see the emotion rising in her

face so he turned away. He couldn't go there. Not now. As he looked over the last of the people in the rotunda, it occurred to him that he hadn't seen Jon in quite a while. Not since he left to go and secure one of the back entrances.

"Where's Jon?"

Sam pursed her lips. "Haven't seen him."

Just when Xander thought it would be impossible to feel anything, he could still feel the pit forming in his stomach. "That's not like him, Sam. He's the president of the United States right now. We have to—"

"Xander!" a man shouted from the other side of the rotunda.

The light was almost gone outside, but when Xander turned around, there was just enough coming into the rotunda for him to see Jon limping in. He rushed over to him. When he got close, he could see blood on his pants. "What the hell happened?"

"From what I hear, the guys that happened to you out front, they also sent some to the back. The others are dead. I barely made it back."

"How bad is it?" Xander said.

The dark blood looked heavily smeared on the outside of Jon's thigh.

"I don't think the bullet stayed in. I'm fine. Everyone okay here?"

Xander swallowed hard. "We lost more than a few."

"Shit. Any leads? Who they are, where they came from?"

"Yeah, a boy led them here. I'll tell you more as we walk," Xander said, then looked down at Jon's leg. "If you can walk."

"I'll be fine. So, you know where we're going?"

"Ford House offices. The kid knows the way."

"I know the building. It's probably a good time to go, too. It's getting dark. That will help us make it there undetected."

"Gear up," Xander said. "Let's get moving ASAP."

Jon nodded. "I'll clean myself up, then I'll be ready to move."

"Copy."

Xander walked over to Natalie and Santi. "My friend knows the way to the office building. If you tell me which office, you can stay back if you feel safer."

Santi looked up. Xander could see worry in his eyes. "I'm just worried about my mom. She has no idea where I'm at. She has to be melting down at this point."

"She probably is, but, no offense, I kinda have bigger fish to fry."

Santi nodded. "I know. Guess that's me saying I'm sticking with you if that's okay. My house is too far away."

"It's not safe with us. But it's not safe here either. Why don't you show me to the man's office, then I'll find someplace safe for you."

"Okay."

"All right," Xander said. Then he looked at Natalie. "Grab as much ammo as you can. No guns for Santi. Frightened friendly fire would be worse than enemy fire. I'll be at the door."

"Okay," she said. She took his hand for a moment. "Can I do anything for you?"

"Just be ready to fight. It's all we've got at this point. I'm going to find someplace safe for the both of you until we get this thing figured out."

Natalie nodded and walked away. Xander moved for the hallway. Every part of him was ready to break down. He could feel it. He was walking on a razor's edge. He knew he had to hold it together until they were all safe. Or until he could make an impact on the situation. He would grieve then. Now was not the time.

Xander walked down the hall once again. He was sick and tired of that building. He was ready to get the hell out of there at any cost. He knew it would hold one of the worst memories of his life, and he was ready to leave it behind.

"Looks like most everyone is gone," Xander said as he walked up to Sam and Lawson.

"It took some coaxing," Sam said, "but we convinced them staying here was suicide."

"Yeah, we left out the part that leaving might be too," Lawson said.

Sam reached her hand forward. She was holding two fully loaded magazines. Xander took them. That made five spares for him, and one in his rifle.

"The kid—Santi—knows where one of the players in this thing has an office. Long story short, Santi overheard the man talking to someone about changing America and yadda yadda. He's gonna lead us there now."

"That's huge," Sam said.

"It's something, at least," Xander said. "But don't count on the guy still being there. He knows Santi heard him, so he probably won't stick around. The 'big guy' Santi was yelling about when he first got here is that man's soldier. His name is Jax. He was sent here to make sure the president was dead. At least we didn't give him that."

"Even if this man isn't there, that doesn't mean it will be a wasted trip. If Santi can get us in his office, we might find something. At least find out who he is."

"Lotta good that will do," Xander said. "It's not like we can Google him. Or call Dbie for help."

Sam let that thought hang. Xander felt a sting inside. Even saying Dbie's name hurt. She was going to be devastated. She and Kyle were thick as thieves.

"You know how far it is?" Lawson said. "The office building?"

"Not sure," Xander said. Then he looked back over his

shoulder. Natalie and Santi were walking up. "How far is the building, Santi?"

"I don't know mileage, but if I would have come here without having to stop and hide a couple of times, it probably wouldn't have taken more than ten minutes, running."

Xander looked back at Lawson. "Probably somewhere around a mile then. Won't take long."

"Let's get going," Sam said.

"Just waiting for Jon."

"Is he all right? I saw him limping."

Xander shrugged. "Sounds like he took a flesh wound maybe? When he was at the back exit. The other guys who went with him didn't make it."

Sam let out a sigh. "I just can't believe any of this. What the hell? I mean, how did we not get any warning about this?"

"Inside job," Lawson said. "It's much easier to cover when you're the ones who are supposed to blow the whistle."

Jon came walking down the hallway. He was still limping as he placed a rifle sling around his neck.

"You okay?" Xander said.

"No. But are any of us?"

"No," Xander shook his head. "So, let's go make some other people not okay."

CHAPTER TWENTY-ONE

As Xander stepped out on the plaza, the air was freezing. He had no idea where his coat, suit jacket, or even his shirt had ended up in all the Capitol Building chaos. Natalie had found him a thick wool overcoat, which helped, but it was almost arctic outside. No sunshine made it worse.

The sun had just dipped below the skyline. There was still a blue hue clinging to the sky, but pitch black was coming in a matter of minutes. The darkness of the city was already astounding. Never in his life had he seen so many buildings so dark. The tactical flashlights on their rifles were useless. The EMP had fried the driver circuits that connected the batteries to the LED lights. Everyone still had their cell phones, but they were useless too. The strength of the EMP pulse fried everything inside of them. They were going to have to be able to navigate the streets without an ounce of light. It wasn't going to be easy.

"You think you can get there in the pitch black?" Xander said.

"I can," Jon said. "I've walked this area enough to know. The question is, will I freeze to death before I get there?"

Xander wasn't ready to joke about death. The fact that they couldn't bring Kyle with them hurt more than he could say. The only thing Sam had said before they left was that they put him in a secure location. Xander didn't hear anything after that.

They walked down the Capitol Plaza steps. They could hear gunfire in the distance. Xander believed at that point there might not be a place to put Natalie and Santi to keep them safe.

"We need to bear right here," Jon said. "Past the Library of Congress."

Xander just let him lead. At the moment, he could still see him. He wasn't sure how long that was going to last. As the light continued to fade, Xander could see a few fires dotting the darkness. A couple of hours without power and people were already turning back to the cave days. If this lasted very long, these city people wouldn't survive. There will soon be a new respect for all the country folk out there who know how to hunt and fish for their own food. A dying art in a modern world.

Xander felt Natalie slip her arm around his. He knew she had to be freezing. Xander kept his head on a swivel, and his gun at the ready. He had no idea how far the gunmen who'd come to the Capitol building could be from them.

As they walked through the frosted lawn, Xander could hear people in the streets. Not words, but their sounds. Moving things, talking to each other, even a baby crying. None of them were ready for what the morning would bring. Which is crazy considering what the day had left behind.

"How will we decipher enemy from civilian?" Sam whispered.

"The same way the enemy will I suppose," Xander said. "Just stay tight. If someone starts shooting, we finish it."

The six of them moved from the grass to the street.

"Okay, fall in line and hands on."

Xander reached ahead and grabbed a piece of Jon's shirt.

"What does that mean, hands on?" Natalie said.

"Grab something of someone in front of you and don't let go," Xander said. "Sam, you take the back. We'll do a check six."

"Copy."

"Everybody secure?" Xander said. "Sound off."

"One," Jon said from the front.

Each of them said their number until Sam finished with a six.

"Stay close. If any of you lose your grip say *grip*, and we'll all freeze. We're going to walk fast, so keep up. Ready?"

Everyone repeated. They were ready.

"Take us there, Jon."

Xander felt Jon's shirt pull a bit as he sped forward. No one said anything, so Xander let his worries go so he could focus on the journey. He tuned his ears to his surroundings. The light was all but gone. Xander felt Jon turn left. It was their first street change. As soon as Xander felt everyone should be through the turn he spoke.

"Check?"

"Six," Sam responded.

All was good. The only thing that really changed in the first couple of minutes was the wind being blocked a bit by buildings, and the smells. Unless you were in a restaurant or a bakery, the city always had its foul odors. Take away your sight, and you could actually sense the odors change from street to street. Some were more garbage, while others were heavier on the sewage. Either way, it wasn't exactly a positive note for city life.

The six of them continued to weave through the dark streets of Washington, DC. Xander felt as though they should be getting close. It had been around twelve minutes, and while they weren't jogging, they were walking at a solid pace.

"Check?" Xander called out.

"Six," Sam returned.

Then Xander heard some commotion behind him. It was Natalie's voice, but he could tell that her head was turned away from him.

"Everything okay, Nat?" he said.

She didn't answer immediately.

"Hold," Xander called as he pulled on Jon's shirt.

"I really think we should keep moving," Jon said.

Xander ignored him. "What's wrong?" he whispered back to Natalie.

"Santi said this isn't the way to the Ford House offices."

"Jon? Did we take a wrong turn?"

"No, the kid is mistaken. I've walked this route many times over the last few years here. Now let's go."

"Santi?" Xander said. "Are you mistaken?"

"I—I don't . . ."

"He doesn't know," Jon said. "Can we move now? I'm freezing, and there are gunmen after us in case you forgot."

Xander had no choice but to listen to Jon. They'd fought together before. Jon wasn't the type to lose his way. And if he did, he would say so. It would be really easy for Santi to get turned around. Xander couldn't see anything at that point. The only thing but black in front of him was a few blocks down. He could see what looked like a fire burning at street level.

Jon moved forward. "Moving."

Xander matched his stride and soon the human train was leaving. "Check?"

"Six," Sam called back.

Whatever street they were on, they were heading straight for what looked to be a small fire. Xander was so in tune with his surroundings that he noticed the sound of Jon's footsteps in front of him had changed from when they first started. The cadence was different. Before it was more *step-step step-step*. Now it was more of a normal *step, step, step, step*. Almost as if he'd lost his limp.

Xander's first thought was that after moving for so long, at such a quick pace, maybe his muscle had loosened up. Then his skeptical operator brain kicked in. Before he knew it, three things that had happened with Jon in the last thirty minutes, that alone would seem like nothing, but put together with a pessimistic view, it made Xander's lizard brain twitch.

They were getting close to the fire now. It was almost as if that was Jon's destination. Santis saying they were going the wrong way rang in Xander's head. Then Jon being gone for so long while they were getting ambushed out on the plaza earlier crept in. Also, how convenient it was that Jon came back alone, even though he took two other men with him. The last thought before Xander's gut screamed at him was how the blood had been smeared on Jon's pants. He didn't remember seeing a hole of any sort, and the blood hadn't pooled like it would if it were leaking from one bullet hole. Mix all of that in with maybe he wasn't really walking with a limp right then, and maybe going the wrong direction? Xander had to listen to his gut and pulled Jon's shirt back.

"Hold!" Xander whisper-shouted.

Xander felt Natalie push into his back.

"Xander we've got to keep moving," Jon said immediately. He even started to pull away, but Xander pulled him back in. "What are we doing?"

"Santi, how do you know this isn't the right direction?" Xander said.

"What?" Jon said. "Xander, what the hell are you doing?"

Xander turned into Jon, re-gripped for the front of his

shirt and pulled him close. He could barely see the whites of his eyes. "What happened to your limp, Jon?"

Jon pushed Xander away with two hands on his chest. "The hell are you talking about, X? You accusing me of something?"

"Do I need to?"

"I can't believe you," Jon said. "After all we've been through."

"So you aren't going to answer what happened to your limp? I can hear you walking differently, Jon. This is what I do."

"What? Accuse friends of crazy shit because something happened to your friend?"

Xander snapped.

He swung and barely caught the side of Jon's temple, then he found his hips with his hands and shot for a take-down. He landed on top of Jon and put his knee to his throat.

"How do you know we aren't going toward the Ford House offices, Santi?" Xander said.

Jon was writhing beneath Xander, but he was pinned.

"If you've got nothing to hide, Jon, then just let the kid answer."

Jon stopped fighting for the moment.

Xander didn't take his weight off of Jon. "Go ahead, Santi."

"Be-because, for the last few minutes, the sound of the river is getting louder. With no city noise it's easy to hear."

Xander understood, but he wanted Santi to explain what that meant. "Why does that matter?"

"Because, from the Capitol Building, you have to walk away from the river."

Xander leaned down and put his forearm to Jon's throat. "Smart kid, Jon."

Jon wiggled and pushed Xander's forearm away. "So what, X. I got turned around. Jesus. What's your problem?"

"Lawson, can you help me with something?"

"Sure."

After a couple of seconds, he felt Lawson feeling around to find him. "Right here. Help me pick him up?"

"3 . . . 2 . . . 1 . . ."

They both lifted Jon up from the ground.

"I can't believe you're doing this, Xander. You're losing it, man."

"Maybe," Xander said. Then to Lawson, "Help me get him over to the fire."

Xander and Lawson moved in unison. There was a fire burning in a trash can. It was giving off enough light that he could see the anger in Jon's eyes. He also knew that something was off. He could just feel it. He had been in the game of reading people for far too long, and this wreaked of someone who had something to hide.

Xander looked at Lawson. His face was glowing orange by the flame.

"Hold him."

CHAPTER TWENTY-TWO

JON FOUGHT AGAINST LAWSON'S GRIP FOR A FEW SECONDS. Xander knew it wouldn't last. He knew from experience that Lawson Raines was no ordinary man. He was strong as a bull. After a bit of thrashing, Jon relaxed.

"Just do what the hell you're going to do."

Xander didn't need Jon's permission, but he did what he was told. He reached down to the right pant leg. The one that had been smeared with blood, and the source of the limp that disappeared. He grabbed the fabric at the thigh with his left hand as he pulled his knife from his pocket. He cut a small slit, put away the knife, and then ripped it open. It came as no surprise when Xander didn't find a bullet wound. Disappointment, but not surprise.

Xander stood and took Jon by the throat. He squeezed with his left hand. Jon gagged as he tried to shake free. Before Xander could say anything, gunfire rang out from the other end of the alley. They were prime targets as they were lit by the flame. Lawson chucked Jon down the alley and Xander pulled Lawson down as the rounds ricocheted into the metal trash bin.

"Stop shooting!" Jon shouted toward the dark end of the alley. "It's your President!"

Sam had already moved into position. She bent her rifle around the corner and fired suppressive rounds. Xander saw Jon whip his head around and look at Sam.

"Stop shooting!"

"Why would you do this, Jon?" Xander shouted. "How could you do this?"

"Xander, we need to go," Natalie said from up the sidewalk.

Xander ignored her. "After all we've been through for our country!"

Xander finally saw the men from the dark end of the alley stepping into the light of the flame. It was too dark to see how many, but he could see that they were there. Jon turned to look at them and held up his hand, telling them to stay back. Then he looked back at Xander.

"That's right, after all I've been through for my country. Look what it got me. A slave for the elite who actually run this war machine. Nothing more. With none of the benefits. Our way of government doesn't work, Xander. It's broken. It needed fixed. And the only way to fix it was to tear it down to the studs. Now we can really make this country special again. Like it was supposed to be."

Xander slumped his shoulders and he began to nod. "Why didn't you just tell me?"

Jon looked surprised. "What?"

Sam whipped her head in Xander's direction. It was clear she was bewildered.

"Yeah, I couldn't agree more. I've lost so many friends, and for what? This money machine? The money machine that only makes a few elite players rich? I don't want to be on the wrong side of history here. I'm just fighting to keep me and my friends alive."

"Xander?" Natalie said.

Jon let out a sigh. "Oh my God, I am so happy to hear you say that. And I couldn't agree more. I mean, your best friend just died, and for what? Right?"

Xander bent over and placed his hands on his knees.

"It's okay, X," Jon said. "Let it out, man."

"Xander?" Sam said. "What the hell are you doing?"

Xander stood and wiped tears from his eyes. He looked right at Sam. "I can't do this anymore, Sam. We've given everything. Kyle gave *everything*!" He let the emotions take over. It was dead silent. The entire city was listening. That's how it felt to Xander. "Our entire lives we've sacrificed it all, Sam. We've lost so many. I almost lost my fiancé twice. My best friend is gone."

"Xander."

"No, Sam. It's too much!" Xander was letting it out.

"Xander, this is not you. This is a terrible day that has become overwhelming."

"Terrible day?" Xander's voice was echoing off the buildings. "A terrible *day*? Sam, I killed my own father. With my bare hands. I'm tired of laughing it off. My best friend is dead. I'm done!"

"Come with me, Xander," Jon said. "Together we can make more than a difference. We can make a change! *Real* change!"

"Jon, shut your mouth right now!" Sam said.

"Come on, X. Come here. I'm sorry I wasn't honest with you from the beginning."

Xander stood up straight. Once again he wiped tears from his face. He looked over at Natalie. "I'm sorry."

"Xander!" Natalie shouted. "Do not listen to him!"

Xander looked at Sam. He shook his head. "I'm sorry, Sam."

"Bullshit, Xander. Snap out of it right now!"

Xander looked at Jon. Jon was waving him in. Xander took a step forward.

"Xander!" Natalie shouted again.

Every time he heard the emotion in her voice, it stung like a knife in his skin. But he had to do this.

"Xander!" Sam shouted again.

Xander was right in front of Jon now. Jon was standing with his arms wide, ready to embrace his fellow soldier.

"Let's go make a difference, X. Let's make sure Kyle didn't die for nothing."

Xander stepped in and wrapped his left arm around Jon. Jon wrapped both arms around Xander. Then Xander brought his right hand up like a flash of lightning, slamming the four-inch blade of his knife right in the middle of Jon's throat.

Xander put his nose to Jon's, looking him in the eye. Making sure Jon was looking back.

"You keep my friend's name out of your mouth, you fucking traitor."

Then Xander twisted the knife and a river of blood flooded from Jon's neck. Jon was positioned facing the fire, so Xander could watch the life leave his body. That also meant he had his back turned to the men at the back of the alley. From their perspective, it still looked like Jon had Xander wrapped in a hug.

Xander was holding Jon up at that point.

"Sam, Lawson," Xander whispered. "Don't move, just listen."

No response.

"I'm going to let go of this knife and put my hand on my rifle. As soon as I say go, let's kill every single one of these bastards. Copy?"

"Copy," Sam whispered.

"Copy," Lawson whispered.

Jon's blood warmed Xander's hand as he held him there.

"Natalie, can you hear me?" Xander whispered.

"I can hear you, baby."

"There is a pharmacy right across the street. You see it?"

"I see it," she whispered.

"While we are shooting, you and Santi get inside. Hide. When we are finished with these men, we'll come back for you. Got it?"

"Got it," Natalie said.

"On three."

Xander let go of the knife. It stayed lodged in Jon's throat. He methodically moved his hand to his rifle. He was still holding Jon up with his left arm. He raised his rifle, pointing it toward the men at the end of the alley. He did all of this behind Jon's body so they couldn't see.

"Go!"

Xander held Jon up like a shield as he fired his M4 into the alley. Sam and Lawson joined immediately, and Xander could see that Natalie was already on the move. The crowd of men were on the fringe of the fire's light, so Xander could only see the men in the front drop.

Then came the return fire.

Xander felt rounds moving Jon as they pelted into the back of his body. Sam was on the right shooting around the building. Lawson was on the left. Xander used Jon as a shield as he moved right. He charging handle locked back as he moved behind the building. He dropped Jon as he ejected his magazine and loaded in a fresh one.

"Cover me!" Xander shouted.

As Xander had been doing his dog and pony show for Jon, he had scoured the area surrounding the fire. There nothing that would burn long enough to track down the gunmen. Plus, if they held lights, they would be magnets for the enemy fire. So, Xander did the only thing he could think to do. He grabbed the trash barrel, turned it over, and began rolling it down the alley.

Xander was running behind it as he pushed. Sam and Lawson fell in behind him, shooting as the edge of the light brightened more and more of the alley. Xander saw a man on his left. He ducked down when Lawson shot him, but he continued pushing. Someone else appeared on the right, and Sam took him down. Then Xander saw the big man. He could tell by the red sling connected to his rifle. There were two big trash dumpsters, one on each side of the alley. Xander gave the trash barrel one last push, sending it rolling forward.

"Take cover behind the trash bins!" Xander yelled. "Don't stop shooting!"

When Sam and Lawson both directed their fire toward Jax, he was forced to duck back behind the building. Xander sprinted forward, jumping the barrel, and ran straight for that side of the building. His adrenaline was running so deep that he almost felt as if he was floating down that alley.

"Xander, stop!" Sam shouted.

It was too late. Xander was pot committed. As he approached the end of the alley, he was running out of light. The trash barrel had turned and crashed against the brick building. But the light carried just enough to see the business end of a rifle swinging out from behind the wall.

Xander dove and caught the barrel of the rifle with both hands. The sound of rounds being fired were deafening, but harmless as they sparked up to the sky. He tried to take the rifle with him as he crashed down onto the concrete, but there was a sharp yank, and the rifle stayed with its owner. They were around the corner from the lit alley now. No light to help guide either one of them.

So, it was easy to see the muzzle flash when the rifle was fired. Thankfully, they were just off to Xander left. Xander jumped to his feet and once again dove for the rifle. This time wrapping his arms around what felt like a tree trunk. Not only was this man's body thick like one, but it was also solid as an oak. So much so, that it reminded Xander of his battle with Lawson Raines a few years ago in Mexico City. Xander sent up a silent prayer that either this man wasn't as tough as Lawson, or if he was, that Lawson made it down that alley to help him . . . real fast.

CHAPTER TWENTY-THREE

XANDER FELT TWO POWERFUL HANDS CLAMP DOWN ON HIS arms, and they ripped his arms away before Xander could lock his hands behind the man's legs. Xander scrambled to get another grip on Jax, but Jax managed to pull Xander upright, then some part of his body slammed into Xander's shoulder. A jolt of pain shot all the way to his fingertips, but he knew he was lucky. Xander knew that blow was meant for his head; it had just been too dark for Jax to see.

Xander spun to try and break free, but Jax felt his movement and slipped his arm around Xander's neck. Xander felt Jax's other arm move to try to cinch up a rear-naked choke, so Xander shot his hand up between Jax's arm and his own neck, just so he could fight Jax's arm from the choke. That's when he felt something hard slam into his chest.

"Get his legs!" Jax said.

Another man had come in to help. Then he felt two sets of hands, one on each of his legs. Even in the chaos, Xander couldn't understand how it was so easy for them to see him and his limbs in the dark. They weren't even fumbling around. They knew precisely where to grab to get his legs. Those thoughts quickly faded when they pinned him to the ground. Xander knew this was it if he didn't have help.

There was a loud bang at the mouth of the alley. That's when the trash barrel, still full of flames, came rolling to a stop. Gunshots at the corner of the building followed. One of the men holding Xander's right leg fell to the ground. Xander used that leg to kick the other man forward. Right into Sam's bullets.

Jax was caught off guard and Xander jumped to his feet. The fire showed several more men behind Jax. But they were all taking cover. Xander threw a left hook at Jax, but he was already on the move. He was forced to dive behind a dumpster to avoid the return fire. Xander's rifle sling had slipped so he had to reach behind his back to pull it around. He joined Sam and Lawson, spraying his 5.56 NATO rounds into the darkness. After a few minutes, there was no more return fire. They either retreated, or they were dead. Xander was hoping for the latter.

The three of them held their positions. There were noises, cries, and screams from within the walls that surrounded them. The people of DC had to be out of their minds in fear. Xander waited another long minute. There were plenty of sounds, but it was hard to decipher if it was the men who were shooting at them. The fire in the trash barrel was dying, but there was enough light to see one of the fallen men Sam or Lawson had shot. He had something on his head.

Xander grabbed the dead man by the foot and pulled him over. The man was wearing night-vision goggles. Xander was no EMP expert, but all the information and training he'd had on them said that if the electromagnetic pulse was strong enough, like the one over DC had been, even small electronics would be fried.

Sam and Lawson walked up as Xander examined the man's goggles.

"How the hell did they manage that?" Lawson said.

"That's what I was just asking myself," Xander said.

"They knew this was coming, yeah?" Sam said. "So, they probably had a lot of supplies like this in a Faraday cage. That must have protected some of what they are using from the blast. It's the only thing that makes sense."

"Do they all have them?" Lawson said.

"Let's find out," Xander said. He pulled the goggles over his head and went over to the second man who had been holding his leg. He took the goggles off his head. "Here's two." He continued on to a few other bodies lying on the ground. He was hoping to see that Jax was one of them, but he wasn't. "No one else has any."

Xander took a look down the alley. It was bathed in green. There was no one in sight.

"They're gone," he announced as he walked back to Sam and Lawson.

"How do you know we didn't kill them all?" Sam said.

"We might have gotten most of them, no idea, but the big one, Jax, isn't here."

"Okay, so they are headed back to the Ford House offices to report, right?" Lawson said. "We need to get moving."

Xander held the second pair of night-vision goggles out in front of him. The two of them stared at them.

"Don't give them to me," Lawson said. "You two are the tacticians. I'm just the hammer in case you find a nail."

Sam took the goggles.

"Let's get Natalie and Santi, then get moving to the offices," Xander said. "They've probably moved on to the next part of their plan, but we don't have any other leads."

"Outside of losing Kyle," Sam said, "are you all right?"

"I just . . . am."

"I get it. But you were awfully convincing back there."

"I bought it," Lawson said.

"Well, it wasn't all an act. I've had a lot of those feelings throughout my career. But I still choose to believe in this country."

"And what about Jon?" Sam said.

"Nothing surprises me anymore. The guy used to be a good friend and a great soldier. That's how I'll try to remember him."

Lawson laughed. "Yeah, that's probably best. And best we don't talk about any of it, to anyone."

"Why?" Xander said.

"Might not go over well if you tell people you killed the president of the United States of America."

That hit Xander in an odd way. "Damn. I didn't even think about that. But, he wasn't *really* the president."

"Mmmm," Sam mused. "Technically he was."

"Yeah, you're right, Lawson. Maybe we shouldn't talk about any of it."

CHAPTER TWENTY-FOUR

BERNARD CONLEY WAITED, QUITE IMPATIENTLY, IN THE lobby of the Ford House office building. Jax had been gone for quite some time, and he was growing weary. He wasn't overly concerned. If the president was dead, he had control. Jon Vickers had been part of the plan for quite some time. However, Bernard had never been fully convinced how on board he was. That's why he'd told Jax just before he left to make sure Jon didn't make it either. It might be easier to get the public to rally around him, since he was technically an elected official, but Bernard didn't need him. The way things were going, the American people were going to have to fall in line no matter who was in charge.

That wasn't what he had discussed with the other people in his coup. They all wanted Vickers in charge after the takeover. But they weren't here. And it was just better that he himself was in charge. That way nothing would be missed.

After the American people see and hear about the bombs in the cities—the manufactured war—that Bernard and his team were going to *save* them from, they would listen to whoever was protecting them. Fear is more powerful than hope, after all. The only real hurdle he had if both the president and vice president were dead was staying alive himself. The rest of the people at the top of the government food chain would listen to him and his plans to reshape the government. After all, as the Speaker of the House of Representatives, he was the next in the line of succession. Once Jax stops the operator who is making things difficult at the Capitol Building, Bernard knew he could really get down to business on reshaping the government and moving forward.

However, he did not like how long it was taking. Hearing echoes of gunfire throughout the city streets didn't make him feel so confident either. He turned to the security he had with him in the lobby.

"What's going on out there?"

"Not sure, sir, but the last gunshots were heard a few minutes ago. Maybe Jax is on his way back?"

"Is the van ready?"

"Yes, sir, Mr. Conley. We've got it heated up for you."

"And you already sent a couple of teams to the White House, correct?"

"They should be preparing everything for you. The only security on site will be us. Under your command."

"All right. I'm tired of waiting. Let's get over to the White House. Leave someone here to let Jax know we've already gone."

"Copy."

Bernard walked over to the exit and pushed the door open. The icy blast of the cold air hit like a slap, freezing his breath mid-exhale. The VW van was rumbling in the parking lot, the tailpipe sending thick clouds of exhaust fog into the sky. One of his men opened the door. He was close enough to feel the heat wafting from the interior when he heard someone shouting. His men pulled up their weapons and surrounded him.

"Mr. Conley!"

The voice was deep. He'd never heard Jax raise his voice, but he was pretty sure that's who it was.

"We should get back inside the building, Mr. Conley," his security said.

"It's Jax!" the voice shouted. "Don't shoot!"

"It's Jax, stand down."

A second later the security team parted and Jax came around the back of the van, lit in the red brake lights. He had two other men with him. Jax raised his night-vision goggles that they'd had stored in Faraday cages when the EMP hit.

"Please tell me you were just in a hurry to bring me good news?" Bernard said as he looked up at Jax.

"Good news and bad news, sir," Jax said.

"What's the good news?"

"I spoke with Jonathan Vickers at the back of the Capitol Building. I confirmed that the president is dead."

"That is good news. Go on."

"I can also confirm that Vice President Jon Vickers is dead."

"Nice work. Did you catch him off guard?"

"No, sir," Jax said. "We didn't kill him. But I saw who did."

"I suppose the bad news is coming."

"The operator killed him, sir. He must have found out that Vickers was compromised. But Vickers did tell us that his name is Alexander King."

"I've heard the name, but so what? You killed him after he killed Vickers, right?"

Jax shook his head. "He had help. Other operators. We planned the ambush at a trash barrel fire we started when we spoke to Vickers at the Capitol Building. He led them there as we discussed, but King turned on him before we could ambush. Two other operators were with him, and they could shoot."

"Didn't you have plenty of men with you?"

"You split us and sent too many to the White House. But I had King in my hands. I should have killed him. The other two opened fire on us and we—"

"You failed again."

"Yes, sir."

Bernard shook his head. "Listen, Jax, if you want your family to have a place in this new government, you're going to get rid of this problem. It's one man and a couple of people helping. Stop dicking around and kill them. Do you understand?"

Jax nodded. "I do."

"Where are they now?"

"They have civilians with them. I saw the building they ran into. They might still be there if I hurry."

"There you go. Take these men with you and find King. Kill him and everyone with him." Bernard looked around and did a quick count. "There will be eight of you. That should be more than enough, correct?"

Jax nodded.

"No, Jax. I want to hear you say that it is enough, so when you come back, if you have bad news, I'll have you on record. And then we'll have consequences. Don't screw this up."

"Eight is enough, sir. King won't make it, and neither will the people with him."

"Take the other van," Bernard said as he pointed at the other VW bus. "I'll be at the White House. Make it quick."

CHAPTER TWENTY-FIVE

XANDER HURRIED BACK DOWN THE ALLEY TOWARD THE pharmacy where Natalie and Santi were hiding. He had Lawson run in front of him so he could tell him which way to move. The alley was bright green with the goggles on. Sam was on Xander's right. She had a pair on as well.

"Step right to go around Jon's body."

Lawson followed his direction. They continued to jog along the alley. Xander could see the pharmacy just ahead.

"Slow down, Lawson, you're coming to the street. I'll steer you."

Xander sped up and took Lawson by the shoulders. He still felt like he was made of concrete. He moved his hands to steer Lawson to the right. They were jogging right for the pharmacy. Xander pulled him back as they reached the side-walk. They stepped up and over to the door. The glass was shattered by the handle. Xander approached the door and stopped.

"Natalie, it's Xander. We're coming in. Don't shoot."

He pulled, but she had locked the door back. He reached

in through the glass and turned the lock. He pulled the door open halfway.

"Coming in, Natalie!" he said it louder this time, almost at regular speaking volume. "Don't shoot. Do you hear me?"

Xander waited for a second, but never heard anything from her. He pulled the door open the rest of the way and stepped inside. His shoes crunched the glass beneath him. Lawson followed Xander, holding on to his coat, and Sam stayed back at the door.

"Natalie, come on! We need to go!" Xander spoke at regular volume now.

There was no reason she wouldn't have been able to hear him. That nasty old pit was making a comeback as it formed in his stomach. Had Jax circled the block and come back for her? Did she ever actually go inside the pharmacy at all?

"Xander, I think I hear something," Sam said from the door.

"Natalie!" he shouted. Tension was rising. He looked over at Sam. "What is it?"

"Not sure, but it is definitely getting closer. Must be some sort of old vehicle. And it's probably not someone coming to help us."

Xander's jaw clenched. "Natalie!" By that point he had searched the entire first floor. There was a door in the back, behind the counter that he hadn't tried. Just when he was walking toward it, it opened. He raised his rifle, but didn't shoot.

"Xander?" a whisper.

"Natalie?"

"Sshh," she said.

Xander walked over and whispered. "I have night-vision goggles on. Walk with me. Why didn't you come out when I first started calling?"

"I heard people talking just outside. I didn't know who

they were, so I didn't want to move. I think it's just a couple of people who are scared."

"There's a vehicle coming. We need to move."

Xander took Santi by the shoulders. Natalie grabbed his coat.

"They've just turned down this street," Sam said. "The headlights are on. They're coming straight this way. Lawson, come have a look without goggles so I don't have to pull mine off and adjust."

Xander watched as Lawson felt his way around some shelving and back to the door. He could hear the engine now. This was going to be a shootout. Xander lifted Santi off his feet and practically threw him into the back room. He turned and shoved Natalie in that direction.

"Shoot anyone who comes in!" he told her.

He shut the door and turned back to the pharmacy floor. He weaved around the counter and started for the exit.

"They're not slowing down," Lawson said. "Be ready to shoot!"

Xander brought his rifle to eye level and moved down one of the aisles. He could see the light change in his green-tinted goggles. The vehicle was close.

"Look out!" Lawson shouted.

Xander made it around the aisle in time to see Lawson pick Sam up and run with her like a football. A half-second later, his green tint went yellow as a massive crash imploded the front windows of the pharmacy. The front of a vehicle was coming right at Xander. Instinct kicked in and he dove to his right, narrowly avoiding being smashed by the front end of the vehicle. The fender, however, clipped his legs and sent him spinning. He lost hold of his rifle and it hung by the sling around his neck as he crashed into the potato chip rack. His goggles flew off his head and a few of the wire racks poked into his side as he hit.

The fall knocked the wind out of him. He took short quick breaths as he tried to get it back. He was under a pile of chip bags but when he sat up, the light from the headlights was bouncing off the interior walls, so it wasn't impossible to see. He had transitioned to medium breaths as he got to a knee. On the other side of the van, gunfire erupted. It was like being shrunken inside a tin of popcorn. The gunshots echoed all around him. He was still trying to breathe, just as he could no longer hear because of the guns. But he could just barely see the front door of the vehicle open, and he watched a big shadow step out.

Jax.

Xander was gasping for air now. He reached behind him to pull his rifle to the front as he stood, but he caught a boot to the chest that sent him flying backward. So much for catching his breath. He tried to stand, but the same boot kicked his shoulder and put him back down to the ground. Xander's hand landed on some sort of can, and as he turned he chucked it at the shadow. He heard a thud, and this gave him just enough time to stand, and get into a fighting stance.

He still couldn't breath.

The gunfire was still rattling the walls.

The shadow was coming toward him.

It was time for Xander to dig deep, and fight for his life.

CHAPTER TWENTY-SIX

THE GUNFIRE STOPPED FOR THE MOMENT, BUT HE COULD hear his friends fighting for their lives. Xander was glad Jax had found him. Lawson and Sam could probably take care of the rest while Xander kept the big one busy. He finally caught his breath and he felt like a new man.

"Your master send you back here to get rid of the good guys?" Xander said. He was holding his hands up, ready to fight. Jax was about six feet away from him.

Jax didn't say anything, but Xander could see him put his hands in fight position. It was going down.

"You do realize that's what *we* are, right? The good guys? How could you fight for someone trying to ruin our country?"

Jax answered without words. He stepped toward Xander and threw a looping punch. Xander easily parried it and countered with a right hook to the stomach. It landed hard, but Xander thought it probably hurt his hand more than Jax's midsection. Jax moved forward and tried to get his hands on Xander to control him. Jax was smart, that was clear. He knew the leaner Xander would be much quicker. His best chance was to use his strength. But he was too slow, Xander bounced right and kicked where he thought Jax's knee might be. He couldn't see much below the waist. All the light from the headlights stayed higher above the rows of products. His foot connected, but it wasn't solid. He bounced back outside when Jax reached again.

Xander felt like he'd created enough space to have time to get his hands on his rifle. But this time, when Jax lowered his head, he had some extra speed and got his arms around Xander's waist. They both went to the floor. Xander bounced back up, but Jax had gotten a hold of his rifle. He yanked it off the sling, nearly pulling Xander over. Jax turned the rifle in his hand as he stood but Xander kicked up and knocked it out of his hands. That was too close.

Xander went on offense and plowed forward. He lowered his head and tackled Jax at the hips. He drove forward and landed on top of Jax as they hit the ground. Xander darted up Jax's body and straddled him. He brought an elbow down and made contact, but it was dark on the floor, he had missed Jax's head. Jax wrapped both arms around Xander and pulled him down into a bear hug. For the moment, they were at a stalemate.

"Who is it, Jax? Who's doing this, and why are you help-ing? You've clearly spent time in the military. Why are you doing this?"

Jax grunted as he squeezed Xander close, keeping him from rearing back and punching him. "You don't know shit, King. You were just at the wrong place at the wrong time. I was pulled into this shit a long time ago."

Xander didn't understand what that meant. "Pretty sure I was in the right place at the right time," Xander's voice sounded forced, the pressure of Jax's squeeze was tight. "Oth-erwise, the bad guys would have a free run at this thing, wouldn't they? But your master is worried about the guy who fought back at the Capitol. Stop me when I get cold."

"Typical operator," Jax said. "More mouth than fists."

Xander countered those words with three hard punches to Jax's ribs. He knew it wouldn't be enough to make him let go, but he wanted him to feel that Xander was still fighting.

"Enlighten me then," Xander said. "Otherwise, you're just going to die here like all the rest of your mutts they keep sending after us."

The big man had heard enough. He posted up on his elbow and turned Xander over on his back. Swapping positions. Xander tried to reach up to pull Jax close, but he caught a fist to the side of the head. It was a glancing blow, but it was enough to get Xander moving. He pushed Jax away at his hip while he pulled his own legs out through Jax's. He jumped up and threw a punch that landed, then kept coming forward, hitting Jax in the midsection with a solid knee. He was driving Jax backward.

Both of them came to a stop when Jax's back bounced off of what Xander could now see was a van. Jax pushed Xander back and kicked. Xander side stepped it and delivered a fist to Jax's jaw, then a knee to the groin. Jax dropped down to a knee. As Xander was recoiling to throw another punch, Jax landed a hard jab to Xander's left knee. For a second, Xander thought he might have torn a ligament when his knee twisted. He had to take a couple of steps back to see if it was going to hold him. After shaking it out, it felt like it was okay. But it cost Xander. Jax was back on his feet.

Xander could hear commotion on the other side of the van, but he couldn't worry about it. If Jax didn't remain his sole focus, Jax would kill him.

Jax came forward as he pulled his right arm back, so Xander bounced right, the blow didn't land as hard because

Xander was moving away. Staying close let Xander counter. He went low with a right hook to the left kidney. He recoiled and landed a right hook to Jax's left temple. Jax staggered back. Xander moved in, but Jax kicked at the same knee he'd hit a moment ago. Knifing pain shot all the way down to Xander's toes. Then Jax hit him so hard right behind his left ear that he dropped straight to the floor. Jax was on him before he could recover. As a ringing sounded loudly in his ear, Jax grabbed Xander's coat by both lapels and lifted him straight up.

Jax turned left and walked Xander right toward the front window. Before he knew it, Xander was through the glass, and his legs were up over his head as he landed hard on the sidewalk. Shards fell like rain around him. He was disoriented as Jax stepped right through the broken window. He was haloed in red from the van's taillights. Xander tried to stand but stopped when he saw Jax pull out a pistol. He was too far away to make a move.

"Coward," Xander muttered as Jax raised the gun.

Then came the gunshot.

Xander felt nothing.

Nothing at all. Something wasn't right. Xander opened his eyes and saw Jax turning toward the door of the pharmacy and began firing. Lawson ducked back inside. He had shot Jax before Jax pulled the trigger on Xander. Xander surged forward and dove at Jax as he turned his pistol toward him. Another shot rang out, but it also missed. Xander hit him and they went down the sidewalk. Xander went back to punch when Lawson walked up. Xander looked right and Lawson had his gun trained on Jax's head.

"Your friends are dead."

Xander took the gun from Jax's hand.

"Not my men, not my friends," Jax said.

"Who's doing this?" Xander said. "Is it a high ranking

government official? That why they wanted both the president and the vice president dead?"

"I'm not telling you anything."

"Where are they? Ford House offices? The White House? We're going to find them. You might as well clear your conscience before you die and at least do something good."

Jax was quiet. Maybe Xander had hit a nerve. Sam stepped out of the building with Natalie and Santi right behind her.

"Shit," Jax said. "At least let me sit up."

Xander got off of him and saw blood leaking all over the sidewalk. Natalie gasped.

Xander looked up at her. "It's not mine."

It wasn't a small amount of blood. Lawson must have hit Jax when he was holding his gun on Xander. Must have clipped an important part of the body.

Jax let out a sigh. "It's cliché."

"What?" Xander said. "What is cliché?"

Jax winced. "The reason I'm doing this. I never wanted to. But all you CIA and FBI guys are the same. Whatever the man tells you to do, you do it. No matter who you have to threaten or kill."

"You just described you," Lawson said. "You literally killed people, good people, because someone told you to."

Jax winced again, grabbed at his side, and nodded. "Yeah, I did. But not until after they threatened my family. Said they'd kill both my daughters. I knew they meant it. So, what choice did I have?"

"Don't really care," Xander said. "Who's giving the orders. Tell me or I'll shoot you now and find out for myself."

Jax laughed. "You think I'm afraid to die?"

"No, but you're afraid someone will. Two someones that you love. I can make sure they're safe if you tell me what you know."

Jax shook his head. "Everybody always wants something."

"Yeah, crazy, right?" Xander said. His tone dripped with sarcasm. "Imagine a bunch of upstanding people not wanting their country to be overrun by a bunch of communist thugs. Selfish lot, aren't we?"

Jax leaned over and spit a wad of blood onto the concrete. He was dying.

"So was I right? Is it whoever is in succession for the presidency after the president and vice president die?"

Jax let out another sigh.

"That would be the Speaker of the House of Representatives," Natalie said.

Xander looked up at Natalie. She really did love history. Then back to Jax. "That it then? That who it is?"

"Alyson and Maddie," Jax said. "He said he'd kill them both if I didn't help him change the world."

"What's his name?"

"Bernard Conley," Natalie said.

Jax looked up at Natalie, squinted, then smiled. "I must be close to death, cause I swear to God you are that movie star."

"Is she right?" Xander said.

Jax looked back at him and nodded. "There's a lot of powerful people behind him."

"But without him, they would all have to step into the light, right?" Xander said.

"They would. But they wouldn't."

Xander stood and looked at his team. "You heard him. Bernard Conley is their only out. He goes away, they'll have to start on a new plan."

"Please just remember my girls. I'm sorry. Just please remember them."

Xander turned Jax's gun around aimed it at Jax's head. "My best friend is dead because of you and your people.

Apologies if I don't seem overly sorry for your predicament."

Jax started to say something, but Xander shot him right between the eyes. Natalie gasped and turned to cover Santi's eyes.

"Okay, we know who we're going after," Xander said. "I suppose it's up to us to save the world."

Sam let out a sigh as she looked down at Jax's dead body. "What else is new?"

CHAPTER TWENTY-SEVEN

XANDER WALKED AROUND HIS TEAM AND BACK INSIDE THE pharmacy. He was no Washington, DC expert, but he knew the White House was at least a couple of miles from the Capitol Building. On foot it would take them over a half an hour to get there. That's if they hurried.

"I don't think that's gonna work, X," Lawson said. "Maybe we should ponder our next move instead of just jumping?"

Xander turned to face the red glowing Lawson. "What exactly is there to ponder, Lawson?"

"Maybe not trying to stop this tonight with just the three of us. Maybe tonight we take our time to find some allies? There is plenty of military and secret service around here. We can find some friends to help."

Xander put his hands on his hips. "Okay, let's ponder then. Since we haven't seen any good guys come our way in the last eight hours, even though the entire American population knows the president was being sworn in at the Capitol Building today, don't you think that means that Bernard, or Jax, or whoever else they have working with them have already locked down those options? You don't think we would have seen one sign of them by now? Any of them?"

"Okay. I see the logic in that. What about going to CIA headquarters? Start there and find some help?"

Xander scoffed. "You don't think that in all the planning it took to do what they did today, that they didn't have help from the CIA and/or the FBI?"

"Well, I don't know that, X, but I'm just saying, maybe we can find out. Then regroup."

"What do you think this Bernard guy is doing right now? He's sending row after row of his men to try and stop us. You don't think he's in the middle of trying to regroup? Sending scouts out to pull more manpower to the White House?"

Sam walked inside. "If we don't go now and try to stop this, we won't have another chance. Bernard will have absolutely bunkered himself in to that White House by tomorrow morning. Xander, you're right, it's now or never. He's only going to get stronger and more fortified."

Xander and Sam both looked at Lawson. He held his hands up like he'd been caught. "Hey, I didn't say I didn't agree, but a different perspective is always good to check ourselves. Right?"

"Right," Xander said. "And I appreciate it. And I thank you for saving my life a minute ago. But now we've got to get going. Especially if this van won't get us there."

Lawson took another look around the van. "Tires are all intact. We might be able to back her out of here and keep her running. Problem is, they'll see us coming from a mile away."

"Maybe that's a good thing?" Natalie said from the door.

They all turned to face her.

"We're all ears, Miss Storyteller," Xander said.

"You all might be able to kill two birds with one stone. If the van runs. It will drive you over there, and be your distraction. I did a movie once called Traitor. In one of the scenes, they put a cinder block on the gas pedal. While the others got in place, one of them set the cinderblock and pointed the truck at the front of a house. It crashed into the front door, everyone came running to see it, and the rest of the team slipped in the back door behind them."

"I like it," Sam said. "Best idea I've heard yet."

"And the only one," Lawson smiled. "But I like it, too. Question is, who's going to set the van on course at the White House? There are only three of us. Two inside isn't going to cut it."

"I'll set the van," Natalie said.

Xander walked over shaking his head. "Oh, no. Not a chance. I'm not letting you get that close to that kind of danger."

"Xander, I'm pretty sure I have splatters of the president's blood on me. Not to mention I've watched you kill two men, up close and personal, in the last half an hour."

"Yes, but I couldn't help that. You had to be with us. Now you don't."

"She's right, Xander," Sam said. "If she sets the van on course, that gives us three strong players to ambush whoever is waiting at the White House. Now, that still may not be nearly enough, but it gives us at least a thirty-three percent higher chance of surviving."

Xander looked past Sam, right to Natalie. He could tell she had already made up her mind.

"What about Santi?"

Natalie looked back at him and encouraged him to speak up.

"Well, if you don't need me to get you to the Ford House, I think I'll try to get home now."

"By yourself?" Xander said.

"I know these streets. I will be fine."

Xander thought for a moment. "Natalie, you're going to need somewhere to go after you finish with the van. Santi, you can wait at a safe distance, then you two can get to Santi's house and lay low. Santi, you can give me your address, and I'll come back for Natalie when we're done."

Natalie turned to Santi. "Santi?"

He nodded. "Yeah, okay. We can do that."

"You're a brave kid, Santi," Lawson said.

"Let's check the van for supplies before we see if we can get it moving," Sam said. She walked over to the back, pulled down on the handle, then lifted the gate up. Inside there were a couple of extra rifles with some spare mags. Two grenades, and some old towels and rags. "These won't hurt."

Xander walked to the front driver's side door. He opened it and took a seat. Jax had put the bus in park after slamming in. "Here goes nothing!" Xander said as he pushed in the clutch. He wasn't sure which way was reverse so he put it in neutral and started it back up. It came to life. He first tried all the way to the right and down with the gear shift. When he tried to let out the clutch it died. Must have been fourth. He put in the clutch again, and this time brought the gear shift all the way left, then he pulled down. It was loose, but it was in gear. Slowly he let out the clutch as he gave it some gas. The van started to lurch backward. He'd found the right gear.

Xander checked the side mirrors. He found Lawson glowing red and waving his arm to try to help navigate Xander out. Xander eased on and off the clutch and finally, he had it back out into the street. People had started to gather, but they kept their distance. It was a violent scene after all.

Xander pulled the parking brake, put the van in neutral, then got out and walked over to Natalie. She was in front of the headlights. "You know how to drive a stick, right?"

"It's been a while, but yes. It will come back to me."

"It's going to be tricky popping the clutch and getting the block to stay on the gas."

"No it won't," she said. "I'll just drop the cinderblock and let the clutch go. I can jump out of the van."

"I don't like this."

"I know you don't," Natalie said. "I haven't enjoyed any of this today. So let's just do what we have to do to not let the whole world down." She leaned in and gave him a kiss.

Xander raised an eyebrow. "No pressure."

CHAPTER TWENTY-EIGHT

XANDER LET NATALIE DRIVE THE VAN FROM THE pharmacy to a spot a few blocks from Santi's house. It was touch and go at first, but she finally got a handle on it. It was such an old and janky clutch and shifter that any seasoned vet would have struggled. Xander was proud of her.

While she drove, Sam and Lawson geared up. They'd scavenged a few of the dead men around the pharmacy. Picked the rifles and side arms that fit them best, then loaded up on extra ammunition. Sam knew Xander's preferences so she picked for him too. She was handing them up to him as he coached Natalie in the front seat. He was ready to go. Sam made sure to pick up a few things for Natalie as well. Just in case she had some trouble getting to Santi's from the White House.

"My house isn't for another couple of blocks," Santi said.

Xander turned in the van to face him. "I know. Just want to scope things out first. If they know you are the son of someone who works in the building, they may have come to find you here."

Those words scared Santi stiff. "You think my mom is in danger?"

Xander shook his head and kept his voice calm. "No. Just a precaution. We have to be extra careful right now. Even driving this van around when very few other vehicles work in the city is like driving around in an ice cream truck in the middle of summer. It's going to attract attention."

Santi began searching the windows; Xander had worried him. Xander didn't mind. The kid, and everyone else needed to be worried. They needed to stay on their toes. Honestly, it wasn't a stretch at all either. There was a very good chance that some men were dispatched to find Santi at his house.

"How far is the walk from here, Santi?" Xander said.

"It's not far. Just a couple streets over."

"Sam and I are going to walk you there, okay? Nothing to be scared of."

Santi just nodded. He was nervous.

Xander turned to Lawson on back in the van. "Keep an eye on my girl and the van, would you?"

"You got it."

Then back to Santi. "You ready to go home?"

"So ready."

Xander leaned over and gave Natalie a kiss. Her lips were soft. Even in all the chaos, just the feel of them brought his blood pressure down a few points. "Be right back."

"Be careful."

Xander nodded to Santi, then to Sam. The three of them got out of the van. After being in the warm interior, outside the van felt like stepping out of a cozy hug straight into a slap from winter itself. Xander felt his body tense with the extreme temperature change. When he looked over at Sam, he could see it had the same effect on her. The kid didn't seem to mind. He was probably too hopped up on adrenaline to feel the sting.

"Okay Santi, we'll follow you. Just take us the least exposed path, that way Sam and I can make sure it's safe."

Santi moved around the headlights of the van and into the darkness. It wasn't late. Xander could see candlelight dotted around the windows of the apartments and houses. Santi mentioned on the way over that he lived in a town-home. Four units connected side by side. Xander and Sam followed him through the dark.

Before they left, they had checked some of the night-vision goggles. They couldn't find any that weren't busted. They were pretty sensitive equipment, so, dodging fists, bullets, and pharmacy-busting vans had taken its toll. Even though the light of the candles from people's homes didn't travel to the sidewalk, it still helped give them bearings on where they were. If Santi was anything like Xander was as a teenager, he didn't need lights to move around in his own neighborhood anyway.

They crossed over a street then headed away from the van's location.

"Tell me when we're close," Xander whispered.

"Okay," Santi said as he kept walking.

They passed a few people out on the street, but they shuffled away quickly once the glow of their cigarettes showed guns strapped to Xander and Sam. It was just too cold for people to be inside. Xander imagined by morning, some would wake up to family members frozen to death. It was that cold.

"It's only three townhomes down now," Santi said.

There was a window just above Santi's head that had a candle sitting in the sill. It seemed to be the side of a town-home. It was rough to the touch so it must have been brick.

"If you follow along the front or back of these, my house is the last one connected to them on the other side."

"Okay, Santi. Let us have a look. Stay put."

Xander felt his way along the brick wall to the front of the townhome. He poked his head around the corner and was surprised to see some light. There was a small group of people standing around an orange flame. Someone had lit a fire pit. Obviously, under normal conditions, it would be way too cold to stay outside. However, Xander guessed it was people trying to help find Santi, and his mother probably couldn't sit still inside the house.

Xander leaned back to Sam. "Some people around a fire pit or something. Probably hoping to see Santi come home. Let's check the back then let him join them."

"Copy. Follow me," Sam said.

They turned and went back past Santi.

"Looks good, Santi, just going to check the back, then you can go."

"Okay."

Sam moved on. Xander had a grip on the back of her coat. She stopped at the edge of the wall. Xander waited.

"Can't see anything back here," she said.

"Let's loop the perimeter then."

Sam moved forward. Xander kept his right hand on his rifle. They continued in the darkness. They could hear the voices of the people on the other side of the building. Toward the end, probably where Santi's house was, Xander could see a flickering light at the back. Probably another small fire pit.

A shadow moved in front of it. Sam froze. This was a very dangerous situation. In all likelihood, this was just a friend or a parent. Sam and Xander had to stay sharp. They were cloaked in darkness so they waited. Another shadow passed. Then another. They were moving from left to right, in the direction of moving around to the front of the house. Sam waited a few seconds longer, then stepped forward.

Then came a scream.

Sam and Xander rushed past the fire and around the wall. They moved toward the front of the townhome with their rifles in firing position. That's when the real screams came. But it was the six people standing around the fire, all shocked to see two people come up on them with rifles.

"Please don't shoot!" a Hispanic woman said as she looked at Xander.

Sam and Xander both checked the perimeter.

"Did you see someone just come from the back of the house before us?" Xander said.

"Yes, my nephews! They didn't do anything wrong, they were just looking for my son. Please, don't hurt us!"

It was Santi's mother. Xander let out a sigh of relief as both he and Sam lowered their weapons.

"You're sure you haven't seen anyone else like us around here?"

"No, sir. Not at all."

"Sorry we scared you." Xander looked past them to the corner of the townhome at the far end. "Santi! Come on out. It's safe! Come around the front!"

The woman's face morphed from fear to confusion.

"It's okay, Santi!" Xander shouted again.

"You know where my son is?"

A few seconds later, Santi stepped into the glow of the fire pit. His mother threw her arms around him and cried tears of joy. Xander was touched. It had been getting difficult to find things worth fighting for, but this was definitely one of those things. Santi's mother finally let go, then she set her sights on Sam and Xander. She was a small woman, but she did her best to get her arms around them both.

"Thank you! Thank you so much for bringing me my baby! Come, we have food inside. You must be hungry."

"Thank you, ma'am, but we have to get going. Quite a bit left to do this evening."

She hugged them again. "Thank you so much!"

Xander actually got a little bit of joy out of the moment. Not because of Santi's mother's reaction, but because of Sam's. She hated this sort of thing. And it was written all over her orange glowing face.

Kyle would have loved it.

CHAPTER TWENTY-NINE

THE ENTRANCE HALL AND ALL THE SURROUNDING ROOMS IN the White House were filled with candlelight. Pools of buttery light melting across the floor, every candle a tiny sun. Bernard had been in the White House far more times than he could count, but he had never seen it so beautiful. Not even during the holidays when it was adorned with thousands of dollars worth of the finest decorations.

There were plenty of people inside even though D.C. was completely shuttered. All of them had been vetted by Bernard's security, all of them preparing for tomorrow's world-altering events. Most of them were tucked away in the myriad offices dotted around the massive building. Busy with their assignments. Bernard wished he'd had something to work on at the moment, instead of standing around, worrying about his disappointing "super soldier" and whether or not he was actually able to do his job.

There were several military minds in the dining hall having dinner. When Bernard asked them about Alexander King, the worry inside him doubled. Apparently, King was America's golden boy. Bernard immediately had the thought that he'd blackmailed the wrong super soldier. Now every minute that passed, that Jax wasn't back at the White House, felt like an hour. It was wearing him out.

"Your drink, sir," a young woman handed him a glass of bourbon.

Bernard wasn't sure how many he'd had that day. He'd switched over from coffee pretty early in the day. At the time, his switch to liquor had been in celebration. Now, it was more to drown his worries. He wasn't happy about that.

He walked over to the front entrance, where a security guard was standing watch.

"Anything?"

"No, sir. No movement."

Bernard gritted his teeth. "Update me as soon as you hear something."

"Yes, sir."

He took a sip of his bourbon. The sip turned into a gulp. Just like that, his glass was empty. Another woman walked over to him from the state dining room.

"Speaker Conley, General Stratton would like a word with you if you have a few moments?"

Bernard nodded. The woman turned around and walked away. He followed. Any distraction would be a good distraction at that point. He walked through the doors into more candlelight. On the long dining room table was an extra-large map, unfurled, with a few uniformed men looking over it.

"Ah, Speaker Conley . . . or, should I say President Conley?"

Bernard smiled. He liked the way that sounded. "Not yet. We'll take care of those ceremonies in the morning. Bernard is just fine.

"All right. Here's the map of the country," General Stratton said as he pointed. His mustache flapped as he spoke and he was wearing more medals than a trophy factory.

"As you can see, I have marked the ten largest cities in the country. Los Angeles, all the way to New York City. All of them have been prepped over the last year. The bombs that are in place will cripple the most important structures in each city. The message that the United States will never be the same will be loud and clear."

Bernard looked over the map. He could see a lot of localized red marks in cities like Houston, Atlanta, Chicago and so on all across the map. The most popular destinations in the country. All known for certain buildings and aesthetics, all about to change forever.

"And what time will this take place?" Bernard said.

"First bomb is set for 9:00am in Atlanta. It will be a chain of devastation to follow across the country."

"All right. So, what did you need from me?"

General Stratton cleared his throat. "Just wanted to go over the final plans, then ask you about the next phase."

"You mean, when do we want to turn the lights back on?"

"Exactly."

"Somewhere around the three-day mark. We have people with all the proper equipment to repair and restore, correct?"

"We do. It was the most difficult part of all of this really. To make sure we had all of the repair parts in place. This EMP, if we hadn't been ready for it, would have knocked the grid down for at least six months to a year."

"Such a powerful country, constantly so vulnerable," Bernard said.

"Not for long, right?"

"Soon we won't have anyone in the world to worry about shutting down our grid. We'll control them all. And of course, do what's best for everyone globally."

General Stratton smiled a shit-eating grin. "Of course, sir."

"Are there any vulnerabilities that we should all be aware of?"

"Not really, Bernard. We have everything covered. I suppose the only weakness is if we are crippled on our forward-facing front."

"How do you mean?" Bernard said.

"Well, our face to the people, I suppose. They are the only ones who can stop this. If they don't have someone— someone like you—that they can trust, telling them how we are going to get through this tragedy, they will rebel. It won't be the masses, because they are easily swayed, but there is a percentage of this country who will fight."

"So the people in this room are fairly important then."

"Essential is a good word."

A little needling poked at the back of Bernard's brain. Jax came back into mind. His mission all the more important now.

"Then the next thing is where us generals step up. Phase three, I guess. Anything changed on that front?"

"No," Bernard brought his mind back to the plan. "Once we bomb the cities, then turn the lights back on, then we can tell the people it was a Russian and Chinese invasion. Their attempt to take the United States. We tell them we fought them off our soil, then we prepare the war machine for what it has been building for, for decades."

"We flatten both countries," General Stratton said.

Bernard nodded. "Then we have free rein over the rest of the world who will be bowing at our feet."

"All systems go."

"Now if you'll excuse me," Bernard said. "I have other matters."

"Yes, sir. We'll continue to wrap this up. And we do have fifty more soldiers coming in from across the river. For when the bombs go off here tomorrow and the chaos begins."

"Good. When will they arrive?"

"Should be any time."

Bernard was hoping for sooner rather than later. He left the dining room and walked back over to the security guard.

"Nothing to report, sir."

"We have men at each entrance, correct?"

"Yes, sir."

Bernard realized he was in the safest possible position he could be in, short of the presidential bunker. He didn't have access to that yet or he would consider it. There were a lot of things that needed to be handed over that a lot of employees weren't around for yet. He hadn't lost all faith in Jax, but he was certainly concerned. His next move was for more whiskey. That would at least calm his nerves until Jax returned.

He was ready for the morning. When everything was locked down. All questions were answered, and the takeover could finally begin.

CHAPTER THIRTY

GETTING BACK INSIDE THE WARM CABIN OF THE OLD VW bus felt like a day at the beach. All he needed was some sand to sink his toes into, and a nice, fruity drink, umbrella and all. Speaking of drinks, Xander was thinking how good one of those would go down just then.

"Everything go okay?" Natalie said.

"He's back with his mom. It was sweet. Sam hated it."

Sam scoffed. "I didn't hate it. I was happy for them. I just hated that I had to be there."

Xander looked at Natalie, what little he could see of her, and smiled. "See, she hated it."

For a brief moment, even though the circumstances were anything but ordinary, Xander felt normal. The image of Kyle lying dead on the cold marble of the Capitol Building quickly erased that. He supposed that was probably his new normal.

Natalie must have sensed his change because she reached over and took his hand.

"Well," Lawson said from the back. "Nothing left to do now but save the world."

Sam laughed. Xander had moved on.

"I need to get back and see my daughter. She's with good people, but this has to be so scary without her dad being around."

Xander had been so wrapped up in himself and the mess they were in that he never even considered Lawson's daughter. "Man, I'm sorry. Must be hard being here."

"Of course," Lawson said. "So we might as well do something great."

Xander sat up. He didn't need a pep talk, but he liked where Lawson was coming from. "Let's get after it." Then he looked Natalie's way. "You sure this is what you want to do? Acting like an agent and performing like one are two completely separate things. No one here will fault you if you go hang with Santi and his family. Get some food, stay warm."

"Absolutely," Lawson said. "You should stay here."

"Oh come on," Sam chimed in. "What are you even saying, Xander? Acting like an agent and being one are actually very similar. We just wing it most of the time. Sounds about like your experience, right, Natalie? You can handle it."

"Exactly," Natalie said.

She sounded confident, but Xander knew she was scared to death.

"Yeah, yeah, Sam," Xander said. "But Natalie doesn't have to do anything she's not comfortable with."

"I'm ready. I'll be fine."

"The brick we picked up is right here behind your seat," Sam said.

"Let's get this over with," Natalie said.

She put the van into gear, started it up, and eased them on down the street.

"You know the way?" Xander said.

"Yes. Just tell me what to do when we get close."

"Will do. Sam, do you think it's best if we stay together as three? Or should we split up and meet in the middle?"

"I think we definitely stick together. Who knows what we'll encounter once we're there. It will be a lot easier for us to adapt to the situation if we have some backup."

"Agreed," Lawson said.

"I think so too," Xander said. "The good thing is, no matter how many gunmen there are, we have definitely thinned the herd over the last couple of hours. They had to expend a lot more resources trying to get us than they accounted for. I can guarantee you that. Now, how much depletion? Don't know, but it's better than if we'd only had the first run of them to deal with at the rotunda this afternoon."

"Doesn't really matter anyway now does it?" Lawson said. "Whether there is three of them, or thirty-three, it doesn't change our approach."

"No," Sam said. "It does not."

"Okay, we are getting close," Xander said. "I think the best place to go in from is Lafayette Square. The trees in the park will hide the van until you're ready to let it run. Then it will be easier for you to disappear into the park once you're out of the van."

"Okay," Natalie said. Then she took a breath. "So, what exactly is the goal of the van? Because, I know there is quite a bit of space between Pennsylvania Avenue and the entrance to the White House. You aren't expecting the van to make it to the door, are you?"

"No. This is just about a distraction. Just getting onto the lawn will draw—hopefully—a lot of men out."

"May I?" Lawson said.

"Of course," Xander said.

"I agree with you, Xander. But it may fizzle a little bit if it's just a van that comes to rest against a tree. With all that's going on, they might hardly notice."

"Okay, what do you suggest?"

"Well, this definitely takes the danger up a notch for Natalie, but—"

"Then it's a no-go," Xander interrupted.

"Excuse me?" Natalie said. "I can speak for myself."

"Natalie, this isn't about what appetizers we are having for dinner. This is what I do for a living. I'm just trying to protect you."

"Xander, we are at a pivotal point in American history, are we not?"

Xander paused for a second. "I know you love history, Natalie, but learning it, and making it, are two totally different things."

"Exactly. Let me hear him out. We can decide together after that. Go ahead, please, Lawson."

"All right. I was just going to say, the distraction would be much better, and probably get more attention and security coming out of the house . . . if it was on fire."

"Yeah, that's not happening," Xander said immediately.

No one said anything for a moment.

"No," Xander said, louder this time. "We are not setting the van on fire and letting you drive it into the White House lawn. That's insane."

"Devil's advocate," Sam said. "What exactly is our alternative, Xander? We need the help. The distraction is essential. If we can get the men outside with no cover, it cuts our danger level in half, if not more."

"And I want to do that for you," Natalie said. "I understand you're scared for me. That you don't want me to get hurt. I get it. But I can go to a place in my head where this is a movie set, and I am just an actress following the script. No actual danger. I can do this. Let me do this for you."

"Except this isn't a movie. One wrong move, you're dead. I like my chances without taking extra chances with your life."

"How many times has my life been in danger because of what you do?"

"Oh shit," Sam said.

"A lot," Xander said. "And I hate it, but right now, what's the point?"

"The point is, you wouldn't be here today, in this mess, if it wasn't for me. Sam wouldn't be here, and neither would Lawson. They had to come save us because I dragged you to that inauguration. It's my turn to help save you from my mess. Whatever happens after that doesn't matter. You owe me the chance to try after all we've been through."

Silence in the van.

Xander hated this truth about their relationship. He knew Natalie was aware of it, he'd just never heard her say it. She had been in so much danger because of him over the years. He was always allowed to rescue her. In this moment, though he hated it, he actually saw her point.

"Fine."

"What?" Sam said.

"Really?" Natalie said.

"Just do exactly what we tell you to do," Xander said. "Nothing more, nothing less. You promise?"

Natalie squeezed his hand. "I promise. But, can we hurry up and do this before I lose my nerve?"

CHAPTER THIRTY-ONE

NATALIE TURNED OFF THE HEADLIGHTS OF THE VW BUS and turned into the grass of Lafayette Square. She followed Xander's directions until they saw some flames lit at the White House out in front of them. She positioned the vehicle in what they all agreed was the middle of the White House. It was pitch black inside the van.

"Okay. Listen close," Xander said. "You should have plenty of time to jump from the van after you set the brick on the accelerator. You'll do that just before the park grass turns into the road. If you jump as soon as you set it, you should be able to stay on your feet. If not, don't forget to roll. Time it right and you'll still be on the grass. Plus, the earlier you set the brick, the more speed the van can pick up before it hits the fence."

"That also gives it more time to go off course, right?"

"It will be fine. Just give yourself a good landing spot."

Sam leaned up. "Give me your hand, Natalie."

Xander couldn't see anything, but he knew Sam had the grenade in her hand. He was picturing what she was saying in his head.

"This is the pin, okay?"

"Okay," Natalie said confidently.

"All you have to do is yank it, and toss it on the floor right as you are jumping out."

"I *really* don't like this," Xander couldn't stop himself from saying it.

The ladies ignored him.

"I can do that. I've got this, Xander."

It was time for Xander to swallow how he felt about it, and just be encouraging. "I know. I know you can do it."

"What's the timeline?" Natalie said.

Sam answered. "When we leave you, we'll move fast. Count to a thousand in your head. This will give us enough time to get in position, and ready to take advantage of your distraction."

"Then get your ass to Santi's house. No stops. Full sprint."

"I will. I'm ready."

Xander opened his door so the cabin light would come on. "It's not too late to reconsider."

"Get your stuff together and go do what you do best."

Natalie leaned over. Xander met her there.

"I love you," Xander said.

"I love you too. See you soon, okay?"

He nodded. "Give us just a minute to gear up."

The three of them got out while Natalie stayed in the driver's seat. Xander walked around the back. He was ready to go. Lawson and Sam were too. He opened the back hatch to have a little light.

"I'm going right. There's a fountain in the middle of the lawn. I'm going to the closest tree to the right of it. You two do the same on the left. We wait till they come out to investigate the van. We wait till they get close. Then we do work. Got it?"

"Got it," Lawson and Sam said.

"It's 1,000. Then she's gonna send it. We have one shot at this. We have to wipe out everyone inside, right?"

"I don't see any other way," Sam said. "They have to be complicit at this point."

"Okay, you guys go get in position. I'll be right behind you."

Sam walked away. He heard her give Natalie a "go gettem'". Then off they disappeared into the night.

"Start counting!" Sam said as she ran off.

Xander started the timer in his head. He shut the van's rear gate, walked around to the driver-side door, and opened it.

"You ready?" he said.

"Go get in position. I've got this."

He leaned in and gave her a kiss.

"Nine-hundred and thirty . . . Nine-hundred and twenty-nine . . ."

With that, he was off. It wasn't but a few strides before he was across the street, then up and over the fence. If they had men patrolling the lawn, they wouldn't have been able to see the three of them by the fence. It was just too dark.

The closer Xander got, however, the torches they had around the White House lent a little light. He could see the white stone of the fountain on his left. He was able to find the tree fairly quickly too and he posted up behind it.

As he counted down, he did a quick check of his weapons. The M4 was locked and loaded. So was his Glock 19. He had a spare magazine for the Glock, and four for the M4. That was over a hundred and fifty rounds to roll with. He was ready. He just hoped everything went right for Natalie.

As he stood behind the tree counting down in his head, all alone, the weight of everything suddenly began crashing down on him. Hard. Every second that quiet crept in, the image of his best friend, dead on the floor, slammed into his mind too. Now it was nothing but quiet. Nothing to distract him, and he couldn't hold back the tears. He had three hundred seconds, and all he could do was hope that was enough time to stop them from flowing.

There was no movement outside of the White House. Nothing at all to take away the sting of the day. His best friend since fifth grade was dead. His Navy SEAL friend for over fifteen years was a traitor. The president of the United States? Dead. The grid had been destroyed and God only knew how many soldiers they killed at the time of the EMP to keep them from fighting back. Or maybe they just replaced their command with their plants. Soldiers would listen to orders. It's how they're trained.

The entire day was absolutely the worst day he'd ever been alive for. It wasn't close. He sobbed into his coat sleeve a while longer. Wishing his friend was with him right then. It was so cold out it felt like if he didn't wipe the tears they would freeze right on his face. Kyle would be laughing at him right now, seeing him in this state. A total wreck.

When his count got under fifty seconds to go, he decided it was time to dry it up. It was time to make sure his friend's death meant something. If Xander was able to save the U.S. from this current threat, it would be because Kyle sacrificed his life to save Xander.

Xander wasn't going to waste the opportunity to make Kyle a hero.

He turned and put his back up against the tree, staring back toward Lafayette Square. His hand was already on his gun. There was just ten seconds to go.

Xander watched the headlights of the van pop on. He had never been so terrified in all his life. His entire world was in the driver's seat of that van. Way out of her depths, but ready to sacrifice it all for what she loved. He was still the luckiest man in the world.

When the engine started, his stomach dropped. Every muscle in his body was tight.

Then the van moved forward.

There was no turning back now.

CHAPTER THIRTY-TWO

THE VAN SHOT FORWARD FROM OUT IN THE SQUARE. IT WAS just a matter of seconds before it was at the edge of the park. Xander's heart was in his throat as he watched. As it approached Pennsylvania Avenue, Xander heard a distinct change in the motor. It all of a sudden sounded like it was at full gas, pedal to the floor.

"She must have dropped the brick," Xander whispered to himself.

The van charged across the street and plowed through the fence. All Xander could do now was pray that she was okay. The van was moving fast. Natalie had done a great job. Just as it was beginning its ascent up the lawn, a massive double blast echoed through the silent night. A ferocious flame reached for the sky as the gas tank blew. If that wasn't a distraction, Xander didn't know what would be. She'd not only managed to get the van onto the lawn, but she got the grenade to blow as well.

Xander turned and put his rifle to his shoulder. The optics were dead from the EMP so he only had his iron sights. They would do just fine. Right on cue, the door opened and men came running out. The van had stopped just short of the fountain. It was a ball of flames.

"Hold," he whispered, somehow trying to speak telepathically to Sam and Lawson.

They did hold. Three men initially came through the door. Then, by the light of the flames, Xander watched three more come around on the left. Sam and Lawson would take them. Xander could get the men running out the door. They slowed up as they grew closer to the flame. Xander was on a knee now, staying low. They were looking all around for who might be lingering, but so far, they hadn't spotted the three of them.

Then someone else walked out the door.

"What the hell is it?" the man shouted.

Xander didn't know why, but he had a strange feeling in his gut that the man at the front door of the White House was the man he was looking for. He trained his sights on him. Just as he was ready to pull the trigger, gunfire erupted from the trees. Sam and Lawson were shooting at the men on the left.

Before the men coming down the middle of the lawn could adjust, Xander moved his sights to the orange glowing figures with nothing to hide behind. He held down the trigger until all three of them were down. He whipped his rifle back up to the door, but the man had already gone inside. More men would be coming.

Xander ejected his magazine and clicked in a spare. It made no sense to move at the moment. They needed to see if more sitting ducks would come waddling out of the White House.

A couple of minutes had passed. No sign of anyone coming out. They were smart enough to know the lawn was covered by people who could shoot. Xander backtracked fifty feet then ran around the back of the van that was still engulfed in flames. He ran up behind Sam and Lawson who were ready and waiting for him.

"Good start," Lawson said. "We cleared six."

"Not bad," Xander said. "Wish we had a little intel on what's inside."

Xander could see Sam grinning at him in the light of the fire.

"What?"

"Natalie did one hell of a job."

Xander couldn't suppress his smile. "She really did, didn't she?"

"She did," Lawson said. "But now what?"

"We all have a grenade, right?" Xander said.

"Yes," Sam answered.

"I say we walk right through the front door, sling some grenades, then do what we do. Without having any schematics of the building, or any satellite showing us where everyone is, I feel like chaos is our friend. Sam, you and I have been in more situations like this than every single soldier here combined."

"We really don't have a choice," she said. "Lawson, you stay behind us. Whatever we don't see, you shoot it."

"I can do that. But, what if there are people in uniform in there?"

"You mean like cops, or soldiers?" Xander said.

"No, I mean like people who run shit. Captains, generals, et cetera. Isn't this where they would gather? You can't have a one-world government without some higher-ups in the military calling the shots, right?"

"You're probably right," Sam said. "But we don't have the luxury of choice. This is the position they have put three of their operators in. Let's go do what they trained us to do."

"God, I love it when you talk dirty, Sam," Xander said. He

could feel the adrenaline rushing in. "Let's not let them take everything we've worked so hard to protect."

Sam responded by changing out her magazine. Lawson did the same. Xander didn't have any idea what awaited inside that building, but whatever it was, he was ready.

Xander readied his weapon. "Let's do this for Kyle."

CHAPTER THIRTY-THREE

XANDER CHARGED UP THE LAWN TOWARD THE WHITE House door. Gunfire came from the roof. He was already committed so he kicked it into a full sprint. There was not way they could have seen men on the roof. The light didn't carry that high. Xander reached the row of bushes at the front walk. He ducked and shot the man standing at the cracked door. Lawson and Sam caught up to him. Xander could see the flames of candles flickering inside.

"Lawson, Sam and I will clear a path, shooting the men we see when we first get in. If our grenades don't help the candles set the house on fire, that's what I want you to shoot. The bigger the flames, the better our chances."

"Copy."

Xander grabbed his only grenade and pulled the pin. He stood and tossed it through the open door. He heard a man scream "grenade" right before it went off. Sam handed him her grenade and he ran for the door as he pulled the pin. The first grenade had bounced to the right side of the entrance, so he waited until he was inside to throw it to his left. Sam was already firing behind him when he hit the floor. He pulled his rifle up and shot the first man running away from the second grenade. The explosion caught two gunmen running in from a different room.

Lawson was doing as asked. He was shooting at candles all along the walls. Flames were already crawling up the curtains. Xander dove over behind the long planter that sat beside the entrance pillars. The cross hall ran horizontally in front of him, and he could see everything. He raised up and shot two men on the right. Sam moved in behind the other stone planter on the left.

Xander motioned for Sam to watch his left. He called Lawson forward with another gesture. When Lawson made it to him, he put Lawson's hand on his coat and moved forward. He stared down his sights as he stepped out into the hall. There was a doorway on the far side; a man with medals pinned to his chest stood in awe. He was also holding a rifle. He hesitated too long. Xander didn't. He fired and watched the man drop, then moved forward with Lawson at his back. He could feel the hot flames burning all around him.

The White House was melting.

Xander couldn't help but think that so were their plans to ruin his beloved country. He moved forward toward the doorway. He stepped over the dead general and fired at the two men who had just run around the corner. There was gunfire back in the cross hallway. Sam had run into more gunmen. Xander figured the men from the roof would be making an appearance soon.

Xander was in the dining room. There was a large map open on the table. He could see red markings all over it.

"Grab that map!" Xander shouted. He stood watch while Lawson gathered it up and stuffed it down his coat. Xander said a short prayer that something on that map would tell the tale of the day, and maybe the plans for tomorrow.

"Hallway clear!" Sam shouted as she moved into the dining room behind them.

Xander moved forward; there was a door on his left. The two men who ran out of the room had gone that direction. He had to move.

"Cover me!" Xander shouted. "I think they're making a run for it!"

"If they get away, Xander, we won't be able to stop this!"

Sam and her ever-present words of encouragement.

Xander sprinted through the doorway. As soon as he turned the corner, he dove to the floor. The bullets from the men waiting nearly ended his run. Sam and Lawson had caught up. They returned fire, giving Xander the chance to hit the back door. He pushed through the door and out onto the veranda. He took the right side of the two sets of sweeping stairs. He only hit a couple of them, he was moving so fast.

The massive half-moon road that was the driveway waited at the bottom. That's when he heard the vroom of an old engine, and saw taillights at the far end of the drive. Xander looked left just in time to see a man holding a gun, but not fast enough to move. He felt a bullet rip through his shoulder. As he dropped to the ground he returned fire. The man fell to the ground.

From the pavement, he could see the vehicle pulling away. Lawson went flying by him, moving much faster than a man his size should be able to. Xander got to a knee, then he felt arms around him, helping him up.

"Are you hit?" Sam shouted.

Lawson jumped into the driver's seat of an old pickup truck. It was either that or an old beat-up van. Xander would have made the same choice. He heard the engine fire up.

"Let's move!" Xander shouted to Sam.

He separated from her and opened the passenger door of

the truck. Sam jumped in and Xander piled in behind her. Lawson hit the gas and rumbled down the driveway. Xander looked down at the tan coat. His shoulder area was covered in blood.

"You're hit!" Sam shouted. "Put some pressure on it!"

"Just worry about the van. I'm fine!" Xander shouted as he rolled down his window. The freezing cold air jumped inside the truck. He rested the nose of his rifle on the windowsill.

"You have to stop the bleeding, Xander. I know it doesn't hurt, that's the adrenaline. That doesn't mean you're not bleeding out!"

Sam was probably right, but he saw the taillights of the van making a right up in front of them and nothing else mattered.

"Right! Right!" Xander shouted.

"On it!" Lawson said as he wheeled the truck right. For a moment, it felt like it went up on two wheels. Then it slid sideways with the turn.

Muzzle flashes came from the back of the van just as bullets ripped through the front windshield. All three of them ducked and the truck swerved, nearly clipping a parked car. Though it felt like a high-speed chase, it was more of a dodging pace, due to all the cars that were on the road when the EMP hit. Some of them had been moved off to the side, but most were sitting right where they went dead.

Xander fired some shots in return, trying to at least make them duck back inside the van. It made a left turn and that's when the brake lights lit up and it came screeching to a halt. Lawson laid on the brakes himself, and they slid to a stop about forty yards from the van. The road they'd turned down was completely blocked with cars. Xander leaned out the window and shot until the two back tires of the van busted.

There was nowhere for the van to go.

Xander got out of the truck and stayed behind the door.

"Come out! There's nowhere to go!"

Silence fell over the city as Xander waited for a response.

CHAPTER THIRTY-FOUR

XANDER WATCHED HIS BREATH PLUME UPWARD IN A FOG AS he waited. The cold air seemed to seep inside his bullet wound. It was an abnormal amount of pain, even for him. Sam stepped out of the pickup truck and stood beside him, her rifle resting on the open window. Lawson mimicked their stance on the other side.

Xander saw something move on the right side of the van. He and Sam both opened fire. A shadow collapsed to the ground.

"All right!" a man shouted. "Okay, hold your fire!"

That was the last thing Xander wanted to do.

"Are you all right?" Sam said to Xander.

"I'm fine." Then, to the unseen man. "Step out away from the van."

"How—how do I know you won't shoot me?"

"You don't. But you have no choice."

"Why are you doing this?" the man said. "We are just trying to regroup after a horrible day. Are you the ones responsible for the EMP?"

"He's playing the victim card," Sam whispered. "You think

it's true?"

Xander shook his head.

"Who are you?" Xander shouted.

"Speaker of the House, Bernard Conley! We think the president is dead, but we have no form of communication. Who are you?"

"Step out away from the van now, or we'll just open fire."

"No, don't shoot. I'm stepping out."

Xander waited. Slowly, he watched as a leg poked out of the van, then two. The man walked into the beams of the pickup's headlights and held up his hands.

"Please don't kill me. I'm the next in line for president. I'm going to do my best to put this country back together."

"Back together from what?" Xander said. "Who did this?"

"We don't know anything yet. Our entire grid is down. No way of communicating with anyone."

"What's the ultimate plan here, Speaker? World domination? That what this is about?" Xander pressed.

"I wish I knew. I don't understand why you attacked the White House. We were forming a plan to try and fight back. Now, we have nothing."

"Speaking of plans, let's look at some. Lawson?"

Lawson walked around the truck and pulled out the maps he'd taken from the dining room table. They were too big to hold, but he got one side open. Xander walked over and had a look at it. It was a map of the United States. Red markings on some of the major cities. He saw a time of 9:00 written beside Atlanta.

"What happens to Atlanta at 9:00?" he asked.

"I-I have no idea."

"Of course you don't." Xander walked over to the man. He could see that he was trembling. Probably a combination of cold and being caught red-handed.

"Please don't hurt me."

"Jax was a tough son of a bitch," Xander said.

"What?"

Xander saw movement in the van. He raised his rifle and just before he pulled the trigger he heard a woman's voice.

"Please, don't shoot! I'm coming out!"

"Susan! Stay in the van!" Speaker Conley shouted.

"I will not! I've had enough!"

An older woman shuffled out of the van. As soon as her feet hit the ground, Speaker Conley started backpedaling.

"Susan, just keep your mouth shut. Everything is fine."

"No, Bernard, everything is not fine." Then she looked at Xander. "He is the man you're looking for. He is the head of the snake for the people trying to ruin this country. I never wanted any of this."

Her voice was shaking. None of it mattered to Xander. He already knew it was the Speaker. However, it would be nice to have someone who had insight into what was happening to tell the people who were actually going to rebuild the government.

Susan went on. "They've got bombs set to go off in every major city tomorrow. There's no way to warn the people. It's already in motion."

Xander felt sick. Here he was with who was responsible, yet there was nothing he could do to stop what was coming.

"Susan, shut the hell up!"

Susan ignored Speaker Conley. "But the real terrible stuff is what was coming after. They were building one government with a bunch of rich oligarchs. But we can at least stop that. I'll never forgive myself but—"

Speaker Conley reached over and punched Susan. "I told you to shut the hell up!" He then jumped on her and started hitting her. Xander rushed over to him and yanked him up with one arm. Lawson was right there to hit him with a right hand to the forehead. He dropped like a sack of sugar.

Susan was crying. "I'm so sorry. I can't believe I was a part of this. He threatened my grandchildren!"

Xander helped her up off the ground and put her back in the van.

"I'm so sorry. I can't believe—"

Xander shut the door so he wouldn't have to hear her anymore. Sam walked over. House Speaker Conley was still lying unconscious on the ground.

"What the hell are we supposed to do now?" Xander said.

That's when a sound in the distance caught their attention.

"Is that a . . ." Sam started.

"Sounds like a car," Lawson said.

"Shit," Xander said as he pulled his rifle up from its sling. His shoulder screamed in pain.

Back behind their truck, they could see headlights coming their way. The three of them braced for a fight. Tires screeched to a halt on the other side of the truck. They couldn't see who it was on the other side.

"Show me your hands!" a man shouted.

"Can't do that!" Xander shouted. "If you have a weapon, put it down!"

"Xander?"

"Natalie!"

"Ma'am, don't go out there!" the man shouted.

"It's Xander!"

"Ma'am!"

A shadow came running around the truck. A second later she nearly took Xander down to the ground. When he caught her, he felt his shoulder slip out of its socket.

"Oh my God, you're bleeding!"

"I'm okay. How are you here?"

A man came walking around the truck.

"I was on my way to Santi's house when he cornered me,"

she said as she pointed back behind her. "Imagine how happy I was to see his badge."

The man walked up, "Alexander King?"

Xander turned to the side to see his face. "Do I know you?"

"No, but we were supposed to have a meeting tomorrow before you left town."

"Steve Bowles? New director of the CIA?"

"Nice to meet you. You wouldn't believe the day I've had trying to fight my way over here."

Xander let out a sigh. "We might have some idea."

Steve looked at Xander's shoulder. Then at Xander. "She told me about your friend. Looks like they hit you too. I'm sorry."

"It's a real shit show."

"You can say that again. Who's that on the ground, and in the van?"

Not sure what the lady in the van does, but she has all the dirt on Speaker of the House, Bernard Conley down there."

"Dirt? I don't understand."

Xander was going to try to explain, but he stumbled instead. Someone caught him before he fell, but he was unconscious before he could see who it was.

CHAPTER THIRTY-FIVE

THERE WAS A BRIGHT WHITE LIGHT, SHINING SO STRONGLY that Xander could see it through his eyelids. At least he thought it was a light. He cracked his right eye open just a hair, but the light was too strong. He didn't hear anything, but he thought he could smell coffee. He tried opening his eyes again, but there was no way he could stare into whatever was beaming at him.

He reached his arm up to shield his eyes.

"He moved!"

Xander heard a woman with a British accent. He was so disoriented that it took him a couple of seconds to realize it had to be Sam's voice. Then he felt arms wrap around him.

"Xander, you're awake!"

"Natalie?"

"It's me. You're going to be okay!"

"Can someone please turn that light off?" he said.

He heard a man laugh. "No lights yet, brother, but I'll close this curtain a bit."

It was Lawson.

Xander could see the shade wash over his closed eyes.

Finally, he could open them. "What the hell's going on?" He looked over and could finally see Natalie.

"We thought we lost you, that's what. Do you remember the last thing you saw?"

Xander took a second. "Were we outside? Didn't the CIA director show up or something?"

"Yeah," Natalie said. "Then you went down. That was three days ago. I'm so glad you're okay."

"Three days," Xander said as he sat up. He felt a little dizzy.

"Go slow," Sam said.

"Yeah, there was no way to get you medical help fast. You lost so much blood. You've been out ever since. With no heart monitors or anything like that, it's been touch and go. But you fought through."

That's when Xander looked over and saw Dbie sitting by the wall. For a moment he had forgotten what happened to Kyle. Seeing her made it all come crashing in.

"I'm sorry I couldn't save him," Xander cried.

Dbie jumped up out of her chair and rushed over to him. She wrapped him in a hug. "Don't say things like that, Xander. They filled me in on what happened. I know you would have done the same for him."

Tears streamed down Xander's face. The pain in his shoulder was nothing compared to what he felt missing his friend.

"I need a minute," Dbie said, and she got up and left the room.

Natalie dried Xander's tears with a tissue.

"I just can't believe he's gone," Xander said.

He felt Sam squeeze his hand. He took a second and gathered himself. "What's going on out there?"

"A lot," Natalie said. "With our help, they found what Speaker Conley was up to. They don't know for sure who he was working with, but they think it's a massive network of people. It's going to be a tough couple of years. They're talking war and all kinds of things."

"What about the cities?" he asked.

Sam shook her head. "We've heard it's bad. Devastating. But we won't truly understand until power is restored."

"When's that supposed to happen?"

"Today, actually," Sam said. "They found that all the parts were in place to replace the blown-out power grid. Apparently they were going to blame China and Russia. Then act like they saved us from them. New World Order and all that conspiracy stuff that doesn't seem like conspiracy anymore."

Xander's head was swimming. He couldn't believe he'd been out so long. "Where are we?"

"In a hotel," Natalie said. "We have some military guarding out front. There are several people within the government staying here that they are protecting. It's been chaos out there. They have finally been able to calm things down by getting word out that power will be restored soon. Four days without electricity and the world falls apart. We might want to rethink how we live going forward.

"We might have to all move out to your horse farm, Xander," Lawson laughed.

"Have you heard from your daughter, Lawson?"

"Yes. She's okay. Some veteran helped me get word to her via Morse code. They tracked her down and let her know I was okay. And she is too."

"Good," Xander said. "Well, thank you all for being here."

"Don't be too mushy about it, X," Sam said. "We've literally nowhere else to go."

Xander laughed. So did everyone else.

"Time is sort of frozen out there at the moment. But it's been nice all being here together," Sam said.

"Speaking of mushy," Xander laughed.

"A lot of things will be different going forward," Natalie said. "But at least we will all have each other."

Xander nodded, but the thought of having each other wasn't the same without Kyle. Nothing would ever be the same. Natalie took his hand and squeezed it. She knew what he was thinking.

What he thought next was inevitable. Was it worth it? Deep down he wondered if what Jon Vickers said before Xander killed him wasn't the truth. Maybe none of it was worth it. The sacrifices of three days ago certainly didn't seem so. At the same time, Xander loved his country. He would literally give anything to keep it safe. Including his own life. So, he felt like that must also mean the lives of his loved ones if he truly meant it.

War machine or not, he still believed the United States of America was the greatest country in the world. He also knew that as soon as he healed, he would be right back out there defending her. For now, though, he was going to rest. Of all the things in the world, he thought he surely deserved that much.

And he would rest. Until she called upon him again.

FALLOUT
by
Bradley Wright
Pre-order book nine in the
Alexander King series today!

ACKNOWLEDGMENTS

First and foremost, we want to thank you, the reader. We love what we do, and no matter how many people help us along the way, none of it would be possible if you weren't turning the pages.

To our family and friends. Thank you for always being there with mountains of support. You all make it easy to dream, and those dreams are what make it into these books. Without you, no fun would be had, much less novels be written.

To my advanced reader team. You continue to help make everything I do better. You all have become friends, and I thank you for catching those last few sneaky typos, and always letting me know when something isn't good enough. Xander appreciates you, and so do I.

About the Author

Bradley Wright is the international bestselling author of espionage and mystery thrillers. War Machine is his thirtieth novel. Bradley lives with his family in Lexington, Kentucky. He has always been a fan of great stories, whether it be a song, a movie, a novel, or a binge-worthy television series. Bradley loves interacting with readers on Facebook, Instagram, and via email. Click on your digital platform of choice below and join in on the fun.

Join the online family:
www.bradleywrightauthor.com
info@bradleywrightauthor.com

Printed in Dunstable, United Kingdom